THE OLD BLUE LINE

A JOANNA BRADY NOVELLA

By J.A. Jance

Joanna Brady Mysteries
Desert Heat • *Tombstone Courage*
Shoot/Don't Shoot • *Dead to Rights*
Skeleton Canyon • *Rattlesnake Crossing*
Outlaw Mountain • *Devil's Claw* • *Paradise Lost*
Partner in Crime • *Exit Wounds* • *Dead Wrong*
Damage Control • *Fire and Ice* • *Judgment Call*
The Old Blue Line: A Joanna Brady Novella

J. P. Beaumont Mysteries
Until Proven Guilty • *Injustice for All*
Trial by Fury • *Taking the Fifth* • *Improbable Cause*
A More Perfect Union • *Dismissed with Prejudice*
Minor in Possession • *Payment in Kind*
Without Due Process • *Failure to Appear*
Lying in Wait • *Name Withheld* • *Breach of Duty*
Birds of Prey • *Partner in Crime* • *Long Time Gone*
Justice Denied • *Fire and Ice* • *Betrayal of Trust*
Ring in the Dead: A J. P. Beaumont Novella
Second Watch

J.A. JANCE

THE OLD BLUE LINE

A JOANNA BRADY NOVELLA

WITNESS
IMPULSE

An Imprint of HarperCollins*Publishers*

Excerpt from *Remains of Innocence* copyright © 2014 by J. A. Jance.

EPub Edition JUNE 2014 ISBN: 9780062366917
Print Edition ISBN: 9780062366924

12

For Dale

THE OLD BLUE
LINE

I KNEW THE two guys were cops the moment Matty walked them over to their booth. I usually work the bar in the afternoons and early evenings, but the daytime cook had turned up sick. In my experience, it's easier and better for my customers to bring in a substitute bartender than it is to bring in a substitute cook. Besides, that's where I started out in this particular restaurant—as a short order cook—and it wasn't much of a hardship for me to be back running the kitchen. As the two newcomers walked past, I had just put up an order and was waiting for Danielle to come pick it up.

Given that the Arizona Police Academy is just up the street, we get a lot of cops at the Roundhouse Bar and Grill. There's always a rowdy crew of newbies—the trainees. They tend to show up in groups and hang out together in the bar in the evenings after class. Next come the instructors. They're mostly older guys, some of them long retired from active police work, who tend to arrive for meals mostly in ones or twos. Not thrilled with retirement, they're glad to get out of their houses for a while and have a chance to hang out in the restaurant, drinking coffee, chewing the fat, and talking over old times.

These two gents looked to be somewhere in the

middle—too old to be trainees and too young to be instructors. They were both middle-aged and severely overdressed for Peoria, Arizona. It may have been the beginning of November, but it was still plenty hot in the Valley of the Sun. These guys were decked out in a way that set them apart from the rest of my regular customers—white shirts, ties, and jackets, the whole nine yards. Yes, and cop shoes, of course. I can spot those a mile away.

After they were seated, one of them said something to Matty—a question, most likely. She looked at me over her shoulder before she answered. When she gave the men their menus, they glanced at them, shook their heads, and immediately handed the menus back. As Matty headed for her hostess station she rolled her eyes in my direction. I knew what she meant. People who come into restaurants at lunchtime and occupy booth space without ordering anything more than coffee are not high on anybody's list in the restaurant biz.

I had taken a new order down from the wheel in the pass-through and was starting on two plates of burgers and fries when my cell phone rang. After answering it, I perched it on my shoulder and held it in place with my jaw so I could talk and still use my hands to cook. It's not easy doing two things at once, but in restaurant kitchens, sometimes you have to.

"They're cops," Matty explained unnecessarily. "Said they'd like to have a word with you."

In my experience, cops who want to "a word" usually want a lot more than that. "What did they order?" I asked.

"They're just having coffee."

"Right," I said. "I thought so. It's lunchtime. In that case, they can take an old cold tater and wait until I'm good and ready to deal with them."

It was almost an hour later before the kitchen finally slowed down. I ventured out into the dining room, wiping my hands on my apron as I went. My overdressed friends were still drinking coffee.

"You wanted to see me?" I asked.

Just then one of my model trains zipped by overhead. In keeping with the Roundhouse name and theme, multiple trains run on tracks laid on a shelf that a previous owner had hung high on the walls of both the dining room and bar. The tracks come complete with tunnel entrances painted on the partition that separates the two rooms. There are three trains in all—two freight and an old fashioned passenger—all of them running at the same time. People often worry about the trains colliding, but they needn't. That's because the shelf holding the tracks is built so close to the ceiling that it's impossible for an onlooker from below to see that there are actually three separate tracks.

"What's the deal with the trains?" one of the visitors asked.

"I happen to like trains," I told him with a shrug, "and so did one of the previous owners. That's why he named the joint the Roundhouse, that and the fact that the bar in the other room is actually round. I was told you wanted to have a word. What about?"

The guy who was evidently the lead reached into

his pocket, pulled out an ID wallet and held it up for my inspection, allowing me to see both his badge and his name—Detective Andrew Jamison of the Las Vegas Police Department.

"I'm Detective Jamison and this is my partner, Detective Shandrow," he explained, pocketing his ID. "We're here investigating the death of a woman named Katherine Melcher."

"Never heard of her," I said.

"I believe you and she were married at one time."

"Then there's some kind of mistake," I told him. "My ex-wife's name was Faith."

"She changed it," Jamison replied. "As I said, her name was Katherine, but she mostly went by Katy."

"She's dead?" I repeated. "Faith is dead? You're kidding. What happened to her?"

"She was murdered, Mr. Dixon," Jamison said. "This is a homicide investigation. Are you sure you want to discuss it here?"

I looked around the room. The biggest part of the lunch rush was over, but there were still plenty of diners in the joint, most of them watching with avid curiosity while the drama played itself out. Behind the counter, Danielle had just clipped another incoming order onto the wheel.

"Sorry," I said. "My cook called in sick. I've got a kitchen to run. The afternoon cook comes on at four. I can talk to you then, but I don't see why I should. What does any of this have to do with me? Faith and I have been divorced for years. She married someone else—my former best friend, actually—so why are you talking to me?"

"Because of this," Jamison said. He reached into his pocket, pulled out a piece of paper, unfolded and handed it over. It was a printed out version of an e-mail. The time stamp said it had been sent on October 15 at 2:00 A.M., Mountain Standard Time, a little over two weeks earlier. I scanned through the text.

Dear Deeny,

If anything ever happens to me, tell them about Butch. He's been calling me lately. He's never forgiven me for leaving him, and I'm afraid he'll do almost anything to get even.

Katy

Deeny. Short for DeeAnn, maybe? I remembered that Deeny had been a grade school chum of Faith's, and I also believed she was an attendant at our wedding, but that was all I knew. Obviously no matter what Faith's name was now, she and Deeny had stayed in touch.

"According to Ms. Hallowell—DeeAnn Hallowell— Katy had complained to her that you were harassing her by phone—that you'd been threatening her."

The whole idea was preposterous. "You think I did this?" I demanded, rattling the paper in the cop's face. "You think I'm responsible for Faith's murder?"

"Are you?" Jamison asked mildly, but watched me

closely as he did so. "Less than a day after Katherine Melcher wrote this, she was dead. Could you tell us where you were on the night of October fifteenth?"

I could barely make sense of it. Faith was dead, but her name was Katherine Melcher now? Who the hell was Melcher? Where had he come from? And what had become of Rick Austin, my supposedly best friend, who had run off with Faith and married her the moment our divorce was final?

I handed Jamison back the computer printout, and that's when I saw the trap because, on the night in question, I had been in Las Vegas attending a mystery writers' convention—a thing called Bouchercon. I had driven up and back, stayed at the Talisman, where I had a coupon, rather than at the convention hotel out on the Strip. I had registered under the name people call me, Butch Dixon, rather than under my real name, Frederick Wilcox Dixon, because I was worried someone would notice the F.W. Dixon connection and think I was somehow related to the woman, masquerading as a man, who wrote all those old Hardy Boys books I devoured as a kid.

If Faith or Katy or whatever her name was now had died that night, and if she had accused me in advance of doing the deed, I knew I was in deep caca.

"Duty calls," I told the two cops. "I've got food to cook. You'll have to excuse me."

I spun on my heel and made for the kitchen. On the way, I stuffed both hands deep in my pockets. I could feel they were shaking, something I didn't want the visiting detectives to see.

At the end of the counter I had to dodge around Matty to get by. "Hey," she said. "Are you all right? Is something wrong?"

"Everything's fine," I muttered as I hustled past her, not much caring if she believed me or not. I snapped the order off the clip and slapped it down on the prep table. Two chili burgers with onions and cheese. I stuck two patties on the grill and stirred the pot of chili that was simmering at low heat over a burner.

Faith was Katy now, and she was dead? Maybe she had changed her name to Katy because she realized the utter hypocrisy of being called Faith while, at the same time, being utterly faithless. Maybe the irony was too much, even for her. I said her new name aloud, just to try it out. "Katy." If I learned to call her that, maybe it would help me maintain the distance I had managed to create between my hurt back then and my new life now.

Dead or alive, I was still a long way from over what the woman had done to me. She had wiped me out— emotionally, financially, and any other "ly" word you care to mention. She had made off with all our savings, maxed out our credit cards, and then filed for a divorce claiming spousal abuse. She had been allowed to stay in our condo on the condition that she keep up the mainte- nance and payments. She didn't, keep up the payments, that is. When she finally got around to selling it, the court decree ordered her to split the proceeds with me. Natu- rally, that didn't happen, either. Instead, she and my good friend Rick lived in our unit rent free for months with- out making any of the necessary payments. They moved out only when they were evicted, having lost the place to foreclosure. In other words, I didn't get a dime.

And then, to add insult to injury, Faith and my mother stayed in touch. More than in touch. They were pals. Even though the ink on the divorce decree was barely dry when Faith and Rick married, my parents nonetheless attended the wedding. Talk about feeling betrayed. Had I still been in Chicago, I think my head would have exploded, but by then I had taken my sad story to my grandmother—my mother's mother—and thrown myself on her mercy.

My grandmother, Agatha, and her daughter, Maggie, could not be less alike. My mother is your basic self-centered shrew. Grandma Hudson, on the other hand, was a wise and loving person—a giving person. She and Gramps had moved to Sun City years earlier, while I was still in school. A few months after they bought a place there, Grandpa took sick and died. Once he was gone, Grandma Hudson announced that she had no intention of sitting around waiting to die. Instead, she went looking for a business to run.

When she bought the restaurant, it was already called the Roundhouse. Having been badly managed, it was a run-down wreck, just up the street from the railroad tracks. She was able to buy it for a song because the previous owner just wanted to get out from under it. At the time, Peoria, Arizona, was a sleepy little burg miles from its boisterous neighbor Phoenix.

Grandma Hudson fixed the Roundhouse up and ran it by herself for ten years. She and Gramps had paid cash for their duplex home in Sun City. Once she bought the restaurant, she rented out the Sun City unit, reserving it as her "toes up" house when it came time for that. Instead, she chose to live in the two bedroom apartment above the restaurant.

By the time Faith finished cleaning me out and I came dragging my weary, demoralized butt to Arizona, Grandma Hudson was eighty-three years old. She took me in as a full partner in the business and let me share her upstairs apartment. Grandma hung around long enough to teach me the ropes before finally turning me loose while she went back to her place in Sun City to relax and retire. The problem is, she had no idea how to go about doing that. Once she hung up her apron and quit working for good, she only lasted three months. When she died, she left me as sole owner of a house I was too young to live in and a bustling restaurant in the middle of what was fast turning into a thriving community.

Matty stuck her head into the kitchen and startled me out of my unseeing stupor. "You might want to take a look at those hamburger patties," she warned. "They're starting to look like charcoal, and they smell worse."

She was right. While standing there lost in thought with the spatula in my hand, I had let the two hamburger patties burn to such a crisp that I'm surprised the smoke alarm didn't go off. I grabbed them off the grill, tossed them into the garbage, and started two more.

Pay attention, I told myself firmly, but that proved to be almost impossible. Once that initial order of chili burgers was up in the window, I called Rocky, the evening cook, and asked him to come in a couple of hours early, so I could deal with the cop issue. Serving decent food is my livelihood. I couldn't afford to turn out slop just because someone was under the mistaken impression that I had knocked off my ex-wife. Fortunately, Rocky lives just over a mile away, so he was there in no time.

Twenty minutes after returning to the kitchen, I walked back into the dining room where the pair of visiting cops had yet to break down and order some lunch.

"How about if we go into the bar," I suggested. "Early afternoons are quiet in there. We'll have a little more privacy."

While leaving the booth, the two detectives didn't bother delivering the money for their check to Matty at the cash register. Instead, they left enough to cover their coffees and a very stingy tip on their table. I was not favorably impressed. Not only were these guys cops, they were cheap cops at that.

The booths in the bar date from a much earlier era. They're Naugahyde cocoons that were built with privacy in mind. I don't much like them because the servers can't see inside them without standing directly in front of the table. The problem is, I don't want to pony up the big bucks to tear them out and start over.

That afternoon, Amanda, one of my cocktail waitresses, was manning—well, womaning, I suppose—my usual bartending shift. She looked up questioningly as we came into the room. I shook my head, letting her know to leave us be. These guys had already spent the better part of two hours occupying one of my booths, with only two cups of coffee to show for the trouble. If they thought

I was going to treat them to something else, they were mistaken.

I was not in a good mood. Faith had left me in a world of trouble when she left me years earlier. This sounded like same song second verse.

"What do you want?" I asked. "And should I have an attorney present for this discussion?"

"It's just a friendly chat," Jamison assured me. "No need to be all hot and bothered."

"I am hot and bothered," I told them. "In fact, I'm downright pissed. My wife left me, wiping me out financially in the process. She ran off with my best friend, cheated me out of my share of the proceeds of our condo, left me in a world of hurt for not paying taxes, and now she's telling the world I'm the one who killed her? Please. If I were going to knock her off, I would have done it years ago—before she let our condo go into foreclosure and before I had to declare bankruptcy just to get out from under the mountains of credit card debt she ran up."

"You sound angry."

"You're damned right I'm angry. Now what do you need from me to get this straightened out? Besides, in cases like this, isn't it always the husband who did it? What about her current husband? What about Rick Austin, her ex-husband and my ex-best friend, who also happens to be a wife-stealing bastard? What about him?"

"Our records indicate that Richard Austin and Katherine divorced three years ago when she first came to Vegas. The timing involved in the move would suggest that she came to Nevada and established residency for the purpose of obtaining a quick divorce from Mr. Austin."

"Well well," I said. "Fair enough. What goes around comes around. Couldn't happen to a nicer guy. So let's cut to the chase. How about telling me what happened?"

"Her husband, Cliff Melcher, reported his wife missing on the morning of October sixteenth when he returned home from a business trip. Her body was found two days later in her wrecked Cadillac Escalade, crashed into a gully northeast of Searchlight. The M.E. tells us she died of blunt force trauma that isn't consistent with injuries due to a car crash. She was already dead when the car went into the wash. So far we have no known suspects, but we're currently investigating all her known friends and associates."

"Including her former husband?"

Jamison nodded.

"Does that mean I'm a suspect?"

"At this point you're a person of interest," Jamison conceded. "One of several, in fact." He paused long enough to pull a tiny notebook and the stub of a pencil out of his jacket pocket. The gesture served notice that our friendly chat was no longer friendly—not in the least.

"Do you mind telling me where you were that weekend?"

There was no point in lying. I had no doubt that these two guys already knew exactly where I was the middle of October.

"I was in Las Vegas," I said, an admission that I had the opportunity to commit the crime. The cops already knew

I had plenty of motive. "I was there for a convention—
Bouchercon."

"What is that exactly?" Jamison asked. "And would
you mind spelling it for me?"

I dictated the spelling and then explained, "It's a convention for mystery writers and readers."

"Which are you," he asked, "a writer or reader?"

"A reader so far," I admitted, "but I'd like to be a
writer someday."

"A mystery writer?"

"Yes."

"As in a murder mystery writer?" From the way he
verbally underscored the word murder in the question, I
could tell exactly what he was getting at.

"I don't know of any other kind," I told him.

I did, actually. There are a lot of different kinds of
mysteries, and I've read them all, from cozies to police
procedurals, from thrillers to true crime, but it's usually
always murder. Right that moment, however, I didn't feel
like giving Detective Jamison an overview of crime fiction. He didn't strike me as the kind of guy who spent
a lot of his time reading books of any kind, much less
mysteries.

"What do people do at this convention?"

"Chat with each other, listen to authors,. go to panels,
visit the booksellers, get autographs."

"What kind of panels?"

The panel entitled "Murder and How to Get Away
with It" had been top on my list of must-sees. The room
had been packed—standing room only. I had also enjoyed

the interview session with the author of *The Poisoner's Handbook*, which turned out to be less of a how-to book and more of a history of the birth of forensic science. I attended both of those, but the thing about Bouchercon is, there's no official sign-up sheet for any of the panels or events. They give you a list of the programs and then you attend the ones that interest you. Once you show up, if there's enough space, you sit. Otherwise, you stand or go somewhere else. It occurred to me that, under the circumstances, I probably shouldn't mention my having attended the panel about getting away with murder.

"I went to several panels," I said, ticking them off one by one. "'Agents: Why You Need One,' 'Is Traditional Publishing Dead?' 'How to Win the E-book Wars,' 'Humor and Murder Do Mix,' that sort of thing."

"Which hotel?"

"The convention was at the Bohemian on the far end of the Strip," I said. "By the time I signed up, I was too late to get the convention price there, so I stayed at the Talisman a few blocks away. One of my customers had recommended it and given me a coupon for one free night."

"Anyone with you on this trip who could verify your whereabouts on the evening in question? Girlfriend maybe, or maybe a gal pal you picked up somewhere along the way?"

I knew what he meant. Jamison was wondering if I had picked up a hooker to keep me company. I hadn't.

"I went by myself," I told him. "Drove up on Friday evening, came back late Sunday afternoon, with no gal pals in the mix at all."

"You drove across Hoover Dam?"

I nodded. Ever since 9/11, they've installed all kinds of security on that road, along with plenty of surveillance cameras, too. If someone went to the trouble of checking the tapes, they'd be able to find me eventually, creeping along in the miserable traffic and driving back and forth in my old beater Honda all by my lonesome. Some day they'll open up that new bridge they're working on—a bridge that crosses the whole canyon. Until they do, crossing the Colorado River at Hoover Dam takes for-damn-ever.

"You said you stayed at the Talisman?"

Recalling the place, I cringed. My customer's idea of "great" and mine don't exactly jibe. The Talisman isn't a hotel I'll be visiting again any time soon.

"Yes," I answered. "It's a few blocks off the Strip, which means it's less expensive, but it was also close enough for me to walk back and forth to the convention. That way I didn't have to pay for parking."

"Do you remember which room you were in?"

"Do you remember hotel numbers weeks after you check out?"

He shook his head. "No," he said. "I suppose not."

"Me, neither," I told him. "Check with the desk. They'll be able to tell you which room I was in. The Talisman is a low-rise hotel. My room was on the second floor, with the swimming pool down below."

"How much did you lose?" Jamison asked.

"I didn't lose," I said. "I went to a convention. I don't gamble in Vegas. The house always wins."

"I mean, how much did you lose when your wife left you?"

"Oh, that," I said. "I lost everything."

And that was the simple truth. I'd had a restaurant off Michigan Avenue. It was called Uptown. At the time, it was a going concern. I had money in the bank, a cool condo close to downtown, and a sizable retirement account. Faith and I also had cars—a late model BMW for me and a Volvo for her. Taken altogether, it added up to more than a mil, including the equity in the condo. When Faith took off with the goods, there wasn't ever any hope of my getting it back. If she and Rick had deposited the money in a bank somewhere, maybe I might have stood a chance of recovering some of it. Instead, it all went up in smoke—literally. It doesn't take long to go through that kind of money when you and your druggie pals are all doing cocaine.

"So how'd it happen?" Jamison asked.

He didn't say, *How could you be so stupid?* He didn't have to. I've said it to myself countless times, but I never saw it coming. Not at all.

I took a deep breath before I answered, remembering back to the first day I ever laid eyes on her.

"Faith showed up in my restaurant one day. She came in at lunch with a guy in a suit and came back later that evening alone. It wasn't long before one thing led to another. She was beautiful as all get out, smart, and charming. I fell for her hook, line, and sinker. She claimed to have an MBA from Fordham, which, I found out later, was bogus, but even without that degree, she knew way more about accounting than I did. After we were married, she was only too happy to take over the bookkeeping and accounting jobs at the restaurant. That's how she met Rick Austin. He was my financial advisor and also my best friend.

"Once they hooked up, the two of them managed to drain my bank accounts—all of them. The first I knew anything at all about it was when I wrote a check to pay the next month's rent on the restaurant, and the damned thing bounced. That's about the time both the IRS and the Illinois tax collectors came calling. Even though I had dutifully signed all the tax forms Faith handed me every year, she hadn't bothered to file them, or to send along the taxes that were due, either.

"By the time I wised up, she had slapped me with a restraining order so I couldn't even go home to get my clothes, couldn't even get into the building to get my car. It was February in Chicago. I had no vehicle, no money, no working credit cards, and the tax men breathing down my neck. Fortunately, I was wearing the sheepskin coat I had bought two years earlier when we went to Vail on vacation. I ended up walking to the building where my former maitre d' lived and crashed on his couch."

"So after she wiped you out like that, I take it you hit her?" Jamison asked. "You were violent?"

"I was not," I replied hotly, feeling my blood start to boil all over again. "I never so much as raised a hand to the woman, not once, but that didn't keep her from claiming I had. She went crying to a local domestic violence shelter with some cock-and-bull story about how I had beaten the crap out of her. They helped her do the paperwork to take out a restraining order and helped her find a shark of an attorney to come after me. I ended up being ordered to pay five thousand a month in temporary support while she and Rick got to stay on in our condo. Of course, with the restaurant shuttered, I couldn't make the support payments. That's when she had me served with papers taking me to court for nonpayment."

"What did you do?"

"The night I got served was the night I hit bottom. I was completely busted. I had gone from having everything to having less than nothing, and here she was threatening to take me to court for not sending her monthly support checks? What kind of deal is that? To drown my sorrows, I drank far too much of my former maitre d's easily accessible booze and very nearly threw myself off his balcony. Ten stories up would have been more than enough to do the job. Luckily for me, I passed out before I could make it happen.

"The next morning, I woke up with a terrible hangover to the sound of a ringing telephone. Grandma Hudson always claimed to be psychic, and maybe she was, because she called me that morning when I was at my lowest ebb. When I had nowhere else to turn, she offered me a lifeline. She told me to wipe the slate clean—to put it all behind me, come to Arizona, and start over. I think it's the best advice anyone has ever given me."

"So that's what you did?" Jamison asked. "You came here?"

"I left town, came to Arizona, and started over from scratch."

"Never tried to get your money back?"

"That would have taken lawyers, and lawyers cost money, which I didn't have. Besides, there was no point. From what I could tell, Faith and Rick had run through most of it by then anyway. Instead, I went to work with my grandmother here at the Roundhouse and lived rent free with her in the apartment upstairs. I filed bankruptcy to get out from under the credit card debt Faith had run up, but that didn't fix my back taxes problem. Grandma Hudson found someone here in town, a retired IRS agent, who helped me cut a deal with the tax man. It took every penny I made for the first three years I was here to pay off the back taxes.

"The restaurant I'd owned before—the Uptown— had been more of a fine dining establishment. Grandma taught me the basics of running your ordinary blue-collar diner. When she died a few years later, she left the restaurant to me—lock, stock, and barrel. By the way, I'm still driving the car she left me, too—an early nineties vintage Honda with very low mileage."

"And when's the last time you saw Kather . . ." Jamison hesitated and then corrected himself. "When's the last time you saw Faith?"

"The day the divorce was final—seven years ago, October thirty-first. It always seemed appropriate that we got divorced on Halloween. I was living in Arizona then, and she's the one who filed. I flew into Chicago the morning of the court appearance and flew back out again that same night. On Halloween, I always allow myself a single trick-or-treat toast in the witch's honor."

"Faith maybe cleaned you out, but it looks like you landed on your feet," Jamison suggested. "After all, you've got all this."

He sent a significant glance and an all-encompassing gesture around the bar, which was starting to fill up. A group of golfers—several foursomes, boisterous, loud, and fresh from some local course—had turned up and were busily making themselves at home by ordering drinks all around, wings, and platters of nachos.

"I already told you. My grandmother owned the Roundhouse, and she left it to me when she died. You may not realize this, but inheriting a restaurant isn't what I'd call 'landing on my feet.' It's called landing in a pile of work. The whole trick about running a restaurant is making it look easy. It isn't. It's like that duck gliding effortlessly across the water without anyone seeing that, below the surface, he's paddling like crazy. By the way, that weekend in Vegas was my first weekend off—my first days off—in months."

"At the time you went there, did you know Faith was living in Las Vegas?"

"I had no idea."

I wouldn't be surprised if my mother had known all about it. I think I mentioned earlier that she and Faith had always been chummy, and it chapped my butt that the two of them stayed friends, especially after what Faith did to me.

"You took your cell phone to Vegas?"

I noticed the sudden shift in direction. "Of course," I answered.

"Did you use it?"

"Some, but on Saturday afternoon I noticed it was running out of battery power and realized I had forgotten the charger back here in Peoria. I called the restaurant, let them know that my cell phone was out of commission. I told them that if they needed to reach me, they'd have to call the Talisman or the people in charge of the convention. At the convention, they post messages on a bulletin board near the registration desk. After that, I shut my cell off and left it off until after I got back home."

I'm not stupid. I could see clear as day where all this was going. Jamison thought I had shut off my phone so it wouldn't ping anywhere near the crime scene. That's how the cops are able to catch the occasional killer these days—by following the bad guy's cell phone signals. That way they can place the crook at the scene of the crime without his ever having made a call.

"My phone records will bear that out," I added.

"I'm sure they will. So did you use the phone in your room to make any calls?"

"No, not that I remember. Besides, who would I have called? Other than the people I met at the convention, I didn't know anyone in Vegas."

"What about the pay phone down by the swimming pool at the Talisman? Did you use that?"

"If there was a pay phone there, I didn't notice, and I certainly didn't use it."

"Who all knew you were going to that particular convention?" This was the first time the other cop, Detective Shandrow, had asked a question.

"The people at the restaurant knew I was going to Vegas," I corrected. "I doubt I mentioned anything to them about the convention. What I was doing in Vegas wasn't any of their business. You know the old saying, 'What happens in Vegas stays in Vegas.'"

My attempt at humor fell flat, at least as far as Detective Shandrow was concerned. He grimaced. "So you're saying that none of the people who work for you are aware that you're building up to writing the great American novel?" His sarcasm was duly noted.

"It's not something I talk about. People don't like it when they think you're standing with a foot in both worlds. They get nervous. I have a good crew working here at the restaurant, and I need to keep all of them."

"Unless you decide to sell," Jamison said.

That took me aback. The truth was, for months there had been considerable interest from a company hot to trot to build a hotel in order to cash in on Peoria's burgeoning Spring Training gold mine. The developer, a guy named Jones, had bought up most of the real estate on either side of me, purchasing the buildings on the cheap from the landlords who had raised the rents enough that their longtime small business tenants—engaged in a life-or-death struggle with big box stores—could no longer afford to renew their leases. Their former landlords were only too happy to make a quick buck and go on to bigger and better things. Now, months later, I remained the sole holdout.

Grandma Hudson was nobody's fool. When she bought the Roundhouse, she bought the whole thing—

both the building and the parking lot, right along with the previous owner's collection of model trains. Once I came on board, I bought more trains, and better ones, too. Unlike some of the other businesses in the neighborhood, I still had a going concern. I also didn't have a money-grubbing landlord trying to bust my balls in order to get me to leave. I hadn't taken the bait at the developer's first offer or even at his second or third.

So yes, I was hoping to sell eventually—at my price—but it wasn't something I discussed out in the open. For one thing, if my crew figured out that I might sell, they'd be gone before the next dinner service, and I'd find myself stuck being chief cook and bottle washer along with having to do everything else. Still, the fact that Jamison and Shandrow knew about my possible real estate dealings meant the two detectives had been hanging around Peoria asking questions for some time, long before they set foot in my restaurant early that afternoon to order their two bottomless cups of coffee.

"Who told you I might be interested in selling?"

Jamison shrugged. "Word gets around," he said.

"I've had some inquiries," I acknowledged. "So far there haven't been any offers out there that I couldn't walk away from. If someone's going to buy the business out from under me, they're going to have to make it worth my while."

"I notice you have a pay phone back there by the restrooms," Jamison said.

This odd observation was completely out of context, but it was also true. Even though pay phones are thin on the ground these days, the Roundhouse has one, and I do my best to keep it in good working order.

"A few of the planned communities around here aren't big on watering holes for the old guys who still like to tipple a bit," I explained. "Some of my regulars are disabled vets who arrive in those handicapped dial-a-van things or else by cab because they're too old to drive or their physical condition makes it impossible. The younger generation may have terminal cell-phone-itis, but not all of the older generation does.

"So yes, I have a pay phone back there so those guys can call a cab or a van when it's time for them to go home. I can also tell you that having a pay phone on the premises is a pain in the neck. When this one breaks down—which it does with astonishing regularity—and stops refunding the change it's supposed to spit back out, people tend to get crabby. They want me to replace their missing change, and most of the time I do. I figure I can afford to lose seventy-five cents easier than some of them can."

"Whoa," Detective Shandrow observed with an ill-concealed sneer. "You're a regular philanthropist."

I wasn't too keen on Jamison, but I liked his partner even less.

"You usually work days, then?" Jamison asked.

"Mostly," I said, "I generally do the day-shift bartending, but because I'm the owner, I pitch in as needed—including serving as short-order cook on occasion, as I did today. I'm here most of the time anyway because I live right upstairs."

"If you don't mind," Shandrow interjected, "I think I'll go use the facilities."

More than ready to be rid of the jerk, I wouldn't have minded if he'd walked straight out the door. He eased his somewhat ungainly body out of the booth and then made for the corridor that led to the restrooms while Jamison put away his notebook and pencil.

"So that's it, then?" I asked.

"For the time being," he told me. "Like I said earlier, we just needed to ask you a couple of questions. Now we'll get out of your hair."

That was pretty laughable in itself because I don't have any hair. When my hairline started receding, I went for the Kojak look and shaved it all off. Jamison stood up just as Shandrow emerged from the hallway. Jamison was between us, and Shandrow was looking at his partner rather than at his reflection in the mirror. I caught the small secretive nod he sent in Jamison's direction. Since neither of them was looking at me at that precise moment, I doubt they realized I had seen it. That nod told me that Detective Shandrow had not only gone down the hall looking for something, he had found it.

"What's the deal with the trophy case and all the photos back there in the corridor?" he asked. "You got yourself one of those dimwit kids?"

I don't have any kids of my own, but I do coach a Special Olympics team, the Roundhouse Railers. When one of my athletes comes into the diner, they always eat for free, and they always want to go visit the trophy case in the restroom hallway. Hearing Shandrow call those sweet folks dimwits left me wanting to punch the man's lights out.

"Those are my athletes." I told him in tight-lipped fury. "And no, I don't have any children of my own, dim or otherwise."

They got the message, Jamison most likely more than Shandrow, and left then, while I stayed where I was. This wasn't a social call. It wasn't my job to see them out. Besides, I was so pissed at Detective Shandrow that I was afraid I'd say something to the man that I'd end up regretting. I was still sitting in the booth when Amanda came over and wiped down the table.

"Who were those assholes, and what the hell was that all about?" she demanded, both hands on her hips. "Were they from down the street?" She jerked her head in the direction of the police academy campus.

"No such luck," I said. "It turns out my ex-wife got murdered, and they're operating on the assumption that I did it."

"Right," she said. "When would you have time?"

"That's what I told them."

"You want something to drink?"

"No," I said. "Not right now. I need to take a run up the road and have a chat with an old friend of mine."

By "up the road" I meant up Highway 60 to Sun City. And by "old friend" I mean old—a spry eighty-two, or, as Tim O'Malley himself, liked to say, "Older than dirt." Tim had retired from the Chicago PD after living and working—much of it as a beat cop—through far too many Chicago winters. He and his wife Minnie had retired to Sun City and, through mere coincidence, happened to own the house next to the one my grandparents bought a couple years later. Tim and Minnie were there for my grandmother when Grandpa Hudson was sick and dying, just as, years later, Grandma was there for Tim during Minnie's slow decline through the hell of Alzheimer's.

And after that? It's difficult to call a pair of octogenarians boyfriend and girlfriend, but that's what they were. Grandma told me once that Tim was far too young for her to consider marrying. They never lived together, either. After all, propriety had to be maintained. Even so, they were good for each other, and over time Tim and I became friends if not pals. Right that minute, I needed some sage advice, and Tim's house was where I went looking for it.

He listened to the whole story in silence. When I finished, he shook his head. "Aggie always said that Faith woman was trouble," Tim commented. "She was of the opinion that anything that looks too good to be true probably is too good to be true. Unfortunately, Faith turned out to be far worse than any of us could have expected."

"I should have expected it," I muttered. "When the gorgeous blonde walks into the room and sweeps the short bald guy off his feet, anyone with half a brain should have figured out something wasn't right. By the time I did, it was far too late."

"Okay, then," Tim said, nodding impatiently. "Enough about her. Let's get back to those cops. Did they come right out and say you were a suspect? Did they read you your rights?"

"No," I answered. "Jamison insisted I was just a 'person of interest,' but I find that hard to believe. They must have been doing some serious poking around in order to learn that I'm considering selling the Roundhouse to that hotel developer. That isn't exactly common knowledge."

Tim nodded again. It was common knowledge to him because I had confided in Tim O'Malley about that, but I hadn't told anyone else.

"How long have these bozos been in town, again?" he asked.

"They didn't say."

"Vegas is a long way from here. It doesn't seem likely that they would have sent two detectives down here to question you if they thought it was some kind of wild goose chase. They must have a pretty good reason to suspect you."

"Yes, but I didn't do it," I insisted. "I had no idea Faith was living in Vegas."

"What about the guy she ran off with?"

"My old pal Rick? She evidently shed him, too, somewhere along the way. I have no idea where he is now."

"What's his name?"

"Austin—Richard Austin."

"He's the guy who stole your wife and your money?"

"I don't think he stole Faith. She probably pulled the wool over his eyes, the same way she did mine, but between the two of them, they both stole my money."

"How much money are we talking about?"

"Over a million," I said.

Tim whistled. "That's a lot of money."

"It is, but once it's gone, it's gone. That's one thing I'm grateful to Grandma Hudson for—she helped me see that it was just money, and water under the bridge besides. In order to get on with my life, I needed to let it go, and I did."

"Cops won't see it that way," Tim cautioned. "Those guys are probably thinking you're still pissed about it."

"Turns out I am still pissed," I corrected. "But not enough to kill her over it. I'm not the murdering type. So what should I do, call a lawyer?"

"Do you have one?"

"No, but . . ."

"You see," Tim said, "here's where those dicks have you by the short hairs. If you don't call a lawyer you look stupid, and if you do call a lawyer, you look guilty."

"What should I do, then?"

Tim considered for a long time before he answered. "For right now, go back to work. Don't stress over this. Stress is bad for your health. Let me see what I can do. I may have been off the force for a long time, but ex-cops have some pull that most civilians don't. I'll get back to you."

He glanced at his watch. He didn't say, *Here's your hat; what's your hurry,* but I got the message and left. When I got back to the Roundhouse, the parking lot was full and so was the bar. The white-haired, blue-plate special folks, sporting their walkers and canes, were wandering into the dining room. That was the other thing I didn't like about selling the place. Any hotel that might replace it—full of polished granite floors and stylish modern furniture—wouldn't be the same kind of comfortable gathering place this one had become for that particular demographic. The new establishment on the block might be slick and cool and hip, but it wouldn't do what the Roundhouse did—remind people of places back home.

I went upstairs, showered, changed into clean clothes, and came back downstairs to the bar to lend a hand. Some of the golfers, a little the worse for wear several hours later, were still there. I told Amanda to collect their car keys and make sure they called cabs before they left. That's when it hit me—all the earlier talk about pay phones. Shandrow hadn't gone down the hall to spend time looking at the Roundhouse Railers' trophy case. He had been in search of the bar's pay phone. I went down the corridor and looked at it myself. I'd had them install it low enough on the wall so it's wheelchair accessible. I stared at it for a long time, but the phone wasn't talking, at least not to me.

Grandma Hudson always claimed work was the best medicine. "It's good for what ails you," she advised me when I came dragging into Phoenix. She must have known how close I was to the abyss. She had insisted that I see a doctor for a checkup, and had seen to it that the doctor prescribed some antidepressants for me as well. Between the two medications—daily doses of hard work and the prescription drugs—I had gradually pulled out of my funk.

That night, the hard work part did the trick again.

The Friday night crowd, larger than usual, was more than I had staffed for, and I helped pinch-hit in the bar. Right around midnight a guy I'd never seen before sauntered into the bar and ordered a St. Pauli Girl, N/A— nonalcoholic—the drink of choice for some of those folks who no longer care to imbibe the hard stuff. The new arrival had the nose of a heavy drinker, and the familiar way he settled his hulking figure on the bar stool told me he had spent plenty of time in bars.

"You Butch?" he asked when I brought him back his change.

"You got me," I answered. "Who are you?"

"Pop told me to look for a bald guy with a mustache," he said. "Had to be you."

"Pop?" I asked.

"Tim O'Malley. My father-in-law—used-to-be father-in-law."

There was a hint of regret in that last phrase. I couldn't tell if the regret came from losing his wife or from losing Tim O'Malley as part of his family.

"Name's Charles," he told me. "Charles Rickover. Charlie to my friends. Me and Amy have been divorced for about ten years now. I still stay in touch with Pop, though. He's a good guy."

I remembered being introduced to Tim's daughter Amy at Minnie O'Malley's funeral. If I'd been told her last name back then, I didn't recall what it was.

"Yes," I agreed. "He is a good guy."

"I used to be a cop," Charles went on. "Put in my twenty. My career came to an abrupt end about the time

Amy left me. Turned out she hit forty and decided she liked women more than men. That was tough on the old ego. I spent some time drowning my sorrows, if you know what I mean."

Wondering where all this was going, I nodded. Had Tim sent Charles by so we could cry on one another's shoulders about the women who had done us wrong? If that was the case, I wasn't exactly in a mood for commiserating.

I had started to walk away when Charles reached into his pocket and pulled out one of those little business card holders. He extracted a card and then lay it on the bar in front of me. When I didn't reach for it right away, he added. "Go ahead. Pick it up. It won't bite."

In the dim light of the bar, I had to pull out a pair of reading glasses to make it out: CHARLES RICKOVER. PRIVATE INVESTIGATIONS. The only other line on the card was a phone number with a 602 prefix. There was nothing else printed there—no address, city, or state, but 602 indicated the business was located somewhere in the Phoenix metropolitan area.

"Pop says he thinks you're being framed for murder and that maybe you could use my help."

I know a little about private eyes—enough to know they don't come cheap. I wasn't of a mind to be bamboozled into hiring one.

"Look," I said, "Tim's a great guy. As I told him earlier, someone knocked off my ex-wife a couple of weeks ago. A pair of cops came by earlier today and asked me a few questions about it. That's all. I never said anything about being framed, and I don't think it's necessary for me to hire—"

"You're not hiring me," Charles said quickly. "I'm doing this for Tim. He stood by me when a lot of other people didn't. When he asks for something, I deliver. He called me this evening and mentioned the framing bit. I still have friends here and there. Between his call and now, I've made a few calls of my own, and you know what? Either you're the guy who did it, and they've got you dead to rights, or else Tim is right, and you are being framed."

"How so?" I asked.

"An old friend of mine happens to work for the Las Vegas PD, and he did some checking for me. It turns out your ex, Katherine Melcher, had received a number of threatening telephone calls in the weeks preceding her death. She had recorded two of the calls—illegally, of course. The person on the phone whispered so it's hard to tell if the caller was a man or a woman. With the right equipment, I'm sure a trained voice recognition expert will be able to sort all that out. Voices are like fingerprints, or so I'm told. The most immediate problem is this—the calls all came from a Phoenix area phone number. Wanna know which one? The pay phone you've got in your hallway there." He pointed with the tip end of his bottle. "The one right outside your crapper."

There was a long pause after that while his words sank into my consciousness. Threatening phone calls to Faith, aka Katy Melcher, had been placed from my pay phone? How could that be?

Charles slammed his empty bottle down on the counter. "Contrary to popular opinion," he said, "I believe you *do* need my help. Your ex may be the one who's dead, but Pop thinks you're the real target, and I tend to agree with him. Given all that, we need to talk. Now where can a guy get a decent cup of coffee around here?"

I walked to the far side of the bar and tapped Jason, my evening and late night barkeep, on the shoulder. "I'm done," I told him. "Will you close up?"

"No prob," he said with a nod.

Beckoning Rickover to follow me, I ducked into the dining room and grabbed the most recently made pot of coffee off the machine behind the counter, then I led the way up the narrow stairway to what is a surprisingly spacious apartment. Because the stairway is situated in the alcove between the dining room and the bar, you enter the apartment in the middle as well.

When it comes to "open concept floor plans," Grandma Hudson was a pioneer. The main room, situated over the restaurant portion of the building, is a combination living room, dining room, kitchen, and office. A master bedroom and bath as well as a guest room and bath are located over the bar. That's not the best arrangement for sleeping, especially on raucous weekend nights, but Grandma probably figured—and rightly so—that whoever lived here would be downstairs working those noisy late nights anyway.

I turned to the right and led Charles into what an enterprising real estate sales guy might refer to as the "main salon." I put the coffeepot on the warmer I keep on the kitchen counter and directed my guest past the plain oak dining table to the seating area in the center of the room. The rest of the place may have been decorated to suit my grandmother's no nonsense, spartan tastes, but the seating area consisted of two well-made easy chairs and a matching sofa. The chintz upholstery may have faded some, but the springs and cushions had held up to years of constant use. With a glass-topped coffee table in the middle, it was the perfect place to put your feet up after spending a long day doing the downstairs hustle.

When I brought the coffee—a mug for Charles and one for me, too, I found him studying his surroundings. "You live here by yourself?" he asked.

I nodded. "Once burned, twice shy."

He gave me a rueful grin. "Ain't that the truth. So tell me the story. Pop told me some of it, but if I'm going to help you, I need to hear the whole thing—from the very beginning."

There's something demeaning about having to confess the intimate details of the worst failures of your life to complete strangers. For the second time in a single twenty-four-hour period, I found myself having to go back over that whole miserable piece of history, but I didn't hold anything back. I understood that if the threatening phone calls to Faith had originated from my place of business, then I was in deep trouble and needed all the help I could get. In that regard, Charles Rickover was the only game in town.

He didn't bother taking notes as I talked. He listened attentively but without interruption as I made my way through the whole thing, ending with a detailed description of my encounter with Detectives Jamison and Shandrow earlier that afternoon. When I went to refill our coffee cups, I returned to find him staring at the office space at the far end of the room. It consisted of an old wooden teacher's desk that Grandma Hudson had liberated from a secondhand store somewhere in front of a bank of used and abused secondhand filing cabinets.

"Is that your computer?" Charles asked, nodding toward my desk and my pride and joy, a tiny ten-inch Toshiba Portégé. The laptop sat in isolated splendor on the desk's otherwise empty surface. Having learned my lesson about allowing other people, namely Faith, handle accounting records for my business, I do those functions myself now, on the computer. The Toshiba also holds the first few chapters of my several unfinished novels.

"That's it," I said.

"Mind if I take a look?"

"Sure."

Charles walked over to the desk, slipped on a pair of gloves, and flipped up the lid on the computer. It lit up right away. He leaned over, studied the screen, and then turned back to me with a puzzled expression on his face. "Dead men don't lie?" he asked.

"It's a story," I explained. "Fiction. It's the title for one of the novels I'm working on."

"You leave your computer sitting here like this?"

I shrugged. "Why not? I'm the only one who lives here."

"You may be the only person who lives here, but you're not the only person who has access."

That was a scary thought and one I had never considered. Since I was downstairs all day, every day, I never locked the place up except on those very rare occasions when I was out of town.

"You're saying one of my people may have been coming up here and messing with my computer behind my back?"

Charles didn't deign to respond. "Tell me about this mystery convention you went to. What's it called again?"

"Bouchercon."

"How did you register for it?"

"On line," I answered, nodding toward the computer. "On that."

Charles sat down in front of the computer and made himself at home. He typed in a few keystrokes. "Yup," he said. "Here it is in your browser history, the Bouchercon Web site. What about your hotel? What was that again, the Talisman didn't you say?"

I nodded. The man may not have been taking notes during my long recitation of woes, but he had clearly been paying attention.

"Is there anything in here about your dealings with your ex?"

I nodded again. "There's a file called Faithless Faith," I said sheepishly. "I thought that writing it down would help me put it in the past."

"Did it?" he asked.

I shook my head. "No such luck."

"Unfortunately," Charles said, "Faithless Faith seems

to have found a way back into your present. What about your dealings with that developer? Are there any records of your dealings with Mr. Jones in here?"

"Yes," I replied. "There have been a number of e-mail exchanges about that."

"In other words, this computer makes your whole life an open book for anyone who cares to take a look-see. Do you happen to have one of those floppy disk drives around here?"

"It's in the top drawer on the right along with a box of extra floppies. I use those to make backup copies of the business records on the computer's hard drive. Why?"

"I want you to come over here right now and make copies of all your essential business files and anything else you want to keep, including those unfinished novels. After that, we're going to reformat your computer. When the cops come back with a search warrant—and I'm saying, when not if—they'll grab your computer and use everything on it to put you away. Not having your files won't stop them, but it'll sure as hell slow them down. Reformatting is the best way to get rid of everything you don't want anyone else to see. If they ask, tell them your computer crashed and reformatting was the only way you could reboot it. You get busy copying your files. In the meantime, give me the keys to your car."

"Why?" I asked.

"Because you're caught up in a complicated plot here, Mr. Dixon," he said, holding out his hand, "and you're about to go down for it."

Reluctantly, I fished my car keys out of my pocket and

handed them over. It seemed to take ages to go through the computer, copying the necessary files. The whole time I was doing so, I couldn't believe any of this was happening. If Charles Rickover was right, one of the people who worked for me—someone I trusted—was trying to frame me for killing Faith. So who was it?

Charles came back upstairs a long time later. He was empty-handed and his face was grim. "Just as I thought," he said. "There's a bloody bat hidden under the mat in the trunk of your car. I believe I have a pretty good idea about where that blood might have come from."

"Did you get rid of it?" I asked shakily.

"Hell no," he said. "I'm pretty sure it's the murder weapon. I'm not touching it, and neither are you."

"You mean we're just going to let the cops find it?"

"Absolutely. In the meantime, you and I are going to do our damnedest to figure out who's behind this."

After returning my car keys, he picked up our empty coffee mugs and went over to the counter where he refilled them. By then I was too stunned to play host. Besides, I was still copying files. Working with floppy disks isn't exactly an instantaneous process.

"Okay," he said, handing me the cup I assumed was mine. "What's in the file cabinets? Are your personal papers there by any chance?"

I nodded. "That's where I keep paper copies of job applications, tax returns, court decrees—bankruptcy and divorce included. That's also where you'll find my birth certificate, Grandma Hudson's death certificate, and a copy of my last will and testament."

"How often do you open those files?"

"Not often, why?"

"With any kind of luck, I think there's a slight chance that those file folders may hold some fingerprints that will work in our favor, unless of course whoever is behind this was smart enough to use gloves. And if the prints are there, the only way they'll work for us is if we can point the cops in the right direction."

"Fat chance of that," I said. "If they come in with a search warrant, I'm toast."

"Not necessarily," Charles said. "While I was downstairs, I called Pop. You've got a guest room here, right?"

"Yes, but . . ."

"Good. Now your guest room is about to have a guest. He's another one of Pop's Sun City chums. His name's Harold Meeks. Thirty years ago he was the top defense attorney in Phoenix, and now he's yours—pro bono, by the way. Pop says Harold's too old to drive or even play golf anymore, but he's still got all his marbles. When it comes to legal maneuvers, he can't be beat. He'll be here as soon as the cab Pop called for him can drop him off. Pop says Harold may need some help getting up and down the stairs, but he'll be here to set the cops straight when they show up with their search warrant.

"Oh," Charles added, "when he gets here, I want you to give him a list of all your employees, both current and former. He'll need to know everything you know about them—approximate hiring dates, where they live, what you know about their personal lives, where they worked before, etcetera."

"Whatever information I have on my employees is on their job applications in the personnel drawer in the filing cabinet."

"Are you listening to me?" Charles demanded. "You are not to go near those filing cabinets under any circumstances! Now, are you done copying your files?"

Properly chastised, I held up a fistful of floppies.

"I'll take those for right now," he said, removing the disks from my fingers and slipping them into his jacket pocket. "Do you know how to reformat that computer?"

"Yes."

"Do it then," he ordered.

I was still reformatting the hard drive—another not-so-instantaneous process—when Charles's cell phone rang. "Okey-dokey," he said. "We'll be right down."

I glanced at my watch as we headed downstairs. It was after two o'clock in the morning. The Roundhouse was closed up tight. The lights were off, the cleaning crew gone. After disarming the alarm, I unlocked the door and opened it. Standing outside, leaning on a walker, was a tiny, hunched over old man with a shock of white hair that stood on end, as though he'd been awakened from a sound sleep and hadn't bothered combing his wild hairdo. If the guy was a day under ninety, I'm a monkey's uncle. Behind him, carrying two old-fashioned suitcases, stood a turban-wearing cab driver.

"I'm Harold Meeks," the old guy announced in a squeaky little voice that reminded me of someone hopped up on laughing gas. "You Butch Dixon?"

I nodded. Harold turned back to the driver. "Okay," he directed. "This is the guy. Give him the bags."

The driver handed them over to me in complete silence, then he retreated to his cab and drove off into the night.

"It's cold as crap out here," Harold griped impatiently. "Are we going inside sometime soon or are we just going to stand here until our tushes freeze off?"

We went inside. As I carried the two suitcases upstairs it occurred to me that my unexpected company obviously intended to settle in for the duration. Behind me, Harold abandoned his walker in favor of letting Charles help him up the stairs. Once Harold was safely deposited on the nearest dining room chair, Charles went back down and retrieved the walker. In the darkened bar downstairs, Harold hadn't looked that bad. Now that I saw him in full light, however, I was shocked. How could this tiny, frail old guy, sitting there in a threadbare sweater and a pair of worn moccasins, possibly be my best hope for beating a murder rap? He looked like he was far more ready to show up for a summons to the pearly gates than for duking it out in an earthly court of law.

"Okay," Charles said, dusting off his hands in satisfaction. "I'm done here and need to head out. I'll leave you two to it."

When it came to my having a capable someone to lean on, Charles Rickover looked a lot more promising than Harold Meeks.

"Wait a minute," I said anxiously. "Where are you going?"

"Vegas," Charles said. "One of Pop's pals is retired Air Force. He keeps a little Cessna over at the Goodyear airport. He doesn't fly at night anymore, but he says we can be wheels up by seven A.M. That means I'd better go home and grab an hour or two of shut-eye."

Charles Rickover bailed at that point, leaving me holding the bag as well as two surprisingly heavy suitcases. "Where's my bedroom?" Harold demanded irritably.

"Down the hall and to the right," I said.

"Good," he said. "Put my stuff in there, then come back and we'll go to work. You got any coffee that's fresher than that crap on the counter? Smells like it's about three hours past its pull-by date."

Which is how I spent the next three hours in the presence of a cantankerous old man who acted as though he'd as soon chew nails as listen to my sad story. Obligingly, I went downstairs to the restaurant, fired up the coffeemaker behind the counter and made a new pot. While I waited for it to brew, I stood leaning against the counter wondering how it was that my fate was now in the hands of this gang of old men—the lame and the halt—who, out of the goodness of their hearts, had joined forces to bail me out of my jam.

I knew Tim O'Malley, the guy Charles called Pop, was responsible. That meant that, by extension, so was Grandma Hudson.

I took the coffee upstairs, only to be ordered back down to retrieve cream and sugar. Since I drink my coffee black, I don't keep cream and sugar upstairs. At Harold's direction, I retrieved a yellow legal pad from the outside pocket of one of his bags. Then sitting at the dining room table, I began telling my story one more time, version 3.0, while Harold took notes, using a Mont Blanc fountain pen to cover one page after another with a totally indecipherable kind of shorthand.

The only time he asked questions was when I was going over what I had said to Jamison and Shandrow. Harold explained that the questions they had asked would probably reveal a blueprint of the kinds of evidence they had against me. As a consequence, I told him everything in the closest thing to word-for-word as I could manage.

Next, I gave him the lowdown on my employees. Again I did it to the best of my ability, but without being able to fall back on the paperwork hidden in those forbidden file cabinets, I couldn't tell him the exact order of hiring, ages, dates of birth, physical addresses, or anything else that seemed to be of much use. Some of my employees, like Matty and Danielle, for instance, are holdovers from my grandmother's day. The most recent hire was Jason, the nighttime bartender, but he always struck me as a straight shooter. Thinking about them one by one, I couldn't focus on a single one that I would finger as the guilty party.

By the time Harold and I finished, it was six o'clock in the morning and I could hear the sounds of people downstairs coming on duty and getting ready to open for breakfast. I was bushed. Harold, on the other hand, was raring to go. It turned out his usual bedtime was five o'clock in the afternoon. So being up and going to work at two o'clock in the morning wasn't exactly a hardship for him. But six A.M. was several hours past his usual breakfast time. I went downstairs and had Maxine cook up a plate of bacon and eggs. "Make that a double order of bacon," Harold told me. "Hells bells, I'm ninety four years old. If bacon's gonna kill me, bring it on, the crisper the better."

I did exactly that—brought him his double order of crisp bacon. In the process, I told my crew downstairs that I was taking the day off. Then, after delivering Harold's breakfast and a fresh pot of coffee, I hit the hay. And slept. A bare three hours later, when Harold Meeks shook me awake, he was totally transformed. Yes, he was still pounding the floor with his walker, but he was dressed to the nines—suit, starched white shirt, and properly tied bow tie. The moccasins had been replaced by a pair of highly polished Johnston & Murphy loafers. His mane of flyaway white hair had been tamed with a layer of gel. He seemed to have shed twenty years overnight and have had a voice transplant.

"Showtime," he announced. "Up and at 'em. I just had a call from a friend of mine who volunteers at the local cop shop. He tells me the search warrant crew is on their way. That's what held everything up—obtaining the warrant. First the cops from Las Vegas had to negotiate a peace treaty with Peoria PD and let them find a warrant-friendly judge, which must not have been very easy bright and early on a Saturday morning. So get a move on. They're probably going to take you into custody, so don't take along anything you don't want stuck in a property locker at the lockup. And remember, I talk, you listen. Do not say a word. Not one. Not to anyone. Not here, not in the patrol car, and not in that jail. Got it?"

I nodded. "What if they try to take your notes?"

He grinned a yellow-toothed grin. "Can't touch 'em," he said. "Attorney/client privilege and all that. Besides, they couldn't read my notes if they tried. It's my own brand of shorthand. I've only had one secretary who could translate it. When Gloria Gray died of a heart attack thirty years ago, that's when I threw in the towel and stopped practicing law. I was too damned lazy to go to the trouble of training someone else."

By then I could hear people storming up the wooden stairway. I sleep in my underwear. Taking my attorney's good advice to heart, I slipped into a set of sweats and a pair of tennies. Then after a quick pit stop, I went to face my doom.

When I came into the hallway, Harold was stationed at the top of the steps, effectively barring any entry. "I'm Mr. Dixon's attorney of record," he told the people waiting outside. He spoke in the stentorian voice that had replaced his earlier squeak, and it was enough to make believers of the new arrivals as he bellowed his instructions. "There is no need for drawn weapons. My client is fully prepared to surrender peacefully as long as you have both a properly drawn arrest warrant as well as a search warrant. Mr. Dixon, by the way, has invoked his right to an attorney. That means you will not be allowed to speak to him outside my presence."

There was a brief pause while documents were exchanged. Harold took his own sweet time examining them.

"Very well," he said at last. "You're welcome to search Mr. Dixon's residence, but everyone involved in the search is required to wear gloves while doing so, lest evidence that might serve to exonerate him be disturbed in any fashion. In addition, anything you take away from here must be treated as evidence. I expect all items to be placed in properly bagged and tagged evidence containers. I'm particularly concerned that any files taken from Mr. Dixon's office be examined for prints. If there is even the slightest indication that the chain of evidence hasn't been properly maintained, there will be hell to pay. Is that understood?"

The response must have been in the affirmative. Having said his piece, Harold pulled his diminutive figure out of the way, and a crowd of cops rushed inside. At the head of the pack were two uniformed Peoria officers, guys who had been in and out of the Roundhouse often enough that I knew them by name without having to peer at their badges. Behind them were two plainclothes Peoria PD guys—one I knew and one I didn't. Bringing up the rear were my old pals, Detectives Jamison and Shandrow.

"Frederick Dixon," the first cop said. "We're placing you under arrest for the homicide of Katherine Melcher. You have the right to remain silent . . ."

While my rights were being read, the second officer went around behind me to fasten the cuffs. "Sorry about this, Butch," he murmured in my ear as he pulled my arms together. "Those guys from Vegas are a pair of pricks."

We certainly agreed on that score, but I took Harold's advice and said nothing. This was serious. Someone was trying to send me up, and my part of the bargain was to keep my mouth shut.

"They'll be taking you to booking, Butch," Harold counseled as we went past. "Again, mum's the word. Trust me. It's gonna be fine."

I nodded, and the two uniformed officers led me down the stairs. The alcove below was crowded with people I knew, workers and customers both. Matty stood in the foreground. With her hands on both hips, she looked like she was ready to take on the cops single-handed.

"It's okay, Matty," I assured her. "This won't take long. You're second in command. It's your job to keep things running until I get back."

"But—" she began.

"Not buts," I said. "Just do it."

"Okay," she said reluctantly. "Will do."

I'd never been booked into anything before. It was a humiliating process. Before long I was printed and changed into my orange jumpsuit. Then they wrapped me in a sort of gray blanket for my mug shot. The whole time, I tried to keep Harold's reassuring words in mind, but that didn't work too well, especially when they put me in a holding cell and locked the doors. The rattle of those jailhouse doors clanging shut and closing me inside sent chills down my spine. And that's when it hit me. Faith had taken everything from me once, and now, even stone cold dead, she was doing it again.

I sank down on the narrow bench that probably

served as a cot overnight. I leaned back against the gray-green cinder-block wall, closed my eyes, and gave in to what was nothing less than a fit of total despair.

They had taken my watch, which I had forgotten to remove, so there was no way to tell how much time passed. An hour? Two? Who knows? I was glad I'd made a restroom stop before all this happened. There was a stainless steel toilet bolted to the floor of the cell, but I resisted the urge to use it. Using it would have made the whole thing more real somehow, and this was already far too real to begin with.

At last a jailer came by—another of the Roundhouse's occasional customers—and opened the door. "Right this way, Mr. Dixon," he said respectfully. "We're going to an interview room just down the hall."

Said interview room would have been crowded with three people in it. With six—the two Peoria detectives, the two guys from Vegas, Harold, and finally me—it was a zoo. Harold seemed to have been transformed into a pint-sized tower of strength, and the local cops deferred to him in a way that made the out-of-towners wince. They, on the other hand, couldn't have been more dismissive.

I found out much later that while all this was happening, on the far side of Peoria a new library building was then under construction, one scheduled to be called the H.M. Meeks Branch. In the hours I'd been cooling my heels in the holding cell, someone inside city government had evidently put the local cops in the know.

"All right, gentlemen," Harold said, as if calling a

business meeting to order. "Perhaps you'd like to tell us what this is all about."

I now know that's an old interrogation trick. You only ask questions to which you already know the answers, and Harold knew exactly what this was about. He already had it down in black and white . . . well, yellow and blue, if you want the exact truth.

Once again the story I'd been forced to tell over and over the previous day came back to me through the mouths of strangers, hinted at more than specified by the questions they asked, which on the advice of my attorney I mostly didn't answer. I could see that was part of Harold's game. He let me answer some of their inquiries— the innocuous ones—here and there, enough to keep the cops interested and enough to keep them asking more questions. All the while, I could tell by the notes Harold made, in that peculiarly indecipherable script of his, that he was gradually gleaning far more about their case than they realized.

An hour or so into the interview, Harold called a halt. Claiming he had a bad prostate, he told them he needed to use the john and suggested that I most likely needed to relieve myself as well. It was more than a need right then. It was straight out desperation, but the Peoria cops assented and allowed as how I'd be able to go to the restroom as long as a deputy accompanied me in and out. The cop stayed back by the door, while Harold and I did our duty at the urinals.

"You're doing great," he told me in a whisper covered

by somebody else flushing a toilet in one of the stalls. "Not to worry."

That was far easier said than done. Back in the interview room, a tray of sandwiches had suddenly appeared, ordered in by Harold. Subway sandwiches have never been my first choice for lunchtime cuisine, but hunger is the best sauce, and I was starved. With all the people marching through my life, it had been more than twenty-four hours since I'd last eaten. Although one of the Peoria guys dissected my twelve-inch tuna/pepper-jack sub before allowing me to eat it, he found no contraband inside, and no escape-enabling metal file, either.

The interview went on for another hour or so after lunch. It ended with Harold laying into Detectives Jamison and Shandrow and letting them know that he would be opposing any efforts made to extradite me to the state of Nevada. After that another jailer led me back to the holding cell area.

The Peoria Police Department has two holding cells. Before I went to the interview, the cell across from mine had been occupied by a pair of drunks peacefully sleeping it off, both of them snoring loud enough to wake the dead. When I returned, the drunks were gone. Now the cells held two new arrivals, a pair of scrawny old guys—both of them north of eighty and both wearing outlandish golf attire. Each was dressed in extremely loud plaid pants with a matching shirt. One was in orange, the other in brilliant chartreuse. They stood at the bars of the cells like a pair of colorful old parrots, yelling at each other across the polished concrete corridor that separated them.

"You're a lowdown cheat," one of them called. "You've always been a lowdown cheat. Why I ever agreed to play another round of golf with you, I'll never know. I saw you move that ball out of the rough, plain as day. The Florsheim club."

"The hell you say," the other replied. "I never kicked a ball in my life. And even if I did, that's no reason for you to come after me with a frigging golf cart. You could have killed me."

"I wish I had. They could have buried you there right on the edge of the fairway under that mesquite tree. It would have served you right. And why the hell did you have to go and crack the windshield of the golf cart with your seven iron?"

"To get you to stop, you stupid old fart!"

"When they come after me to pay for the damages, I'm coming after you, and if you know what's good for you, you'll pay up or else."

Their fight, one that had most likely started on a golf course hours earlier, was still in full swing. No wonder the jailers had placed them in separate cells. From what had been said, I suspected they would soon face charges of assaults with a deadly weapon—a golf cart and a seven-iron, respectively. Any other time that might have been screamingly funny. Not right then.

"Settle down, boys," the jailer cautioned. "You both need to cool off. I understand your attorney should be here soon. He's evidently been delayed."

The jailer opened the door that led into the cell occupied by Mr. Green Pants. The guard ushered me inside and then slammed the door shut behind me. There was that awful, ominous clang again. The metallic noise the locking door made rattled my nerves and chilled my soul. Leaving the two old guys to continue their shouting match, I went over to the stainless steel bench and sank down on it. I had barely closed my eyes when the shouting ceased suddenly as someone walked past me and joined me on the bench.

"You two take your golf way too seriously," I said without opening my eyes. "It's dumb to land in jail over a stupid golf game."

"Well," he said, "look who's talking?"

That actually made me laugh. He was right, of course. Since I was in jail, too, I didn't have much room to point fingers.

"My name's Roger," he said. "And don't worry about Matt and me. Harold will have us out of here in jig time."

"Harold?" I asked. "You mean Harold Meeks?"

"That's the one. He's an old pal of ours. He doesn't play anymore because of his walker, but he usually rides along, drives one of the carts, and helps keep score. He called us when we were about to tee off on the third hole—the par five—after the cops took you away. He asked if I thought Matt and me could figure out a way to get ourselves locked up for the day so we could have a private chat. He said to wait for about an hour, so we staged the whole thing on the par three on the back nine. How'd we do?"

I remembered what Harold had said about not talking to anyone in the slammer. Had the Peoria detectives gone so far as to hire a couple of retirees as jailhouse snitches? That seemed unlikely, but still . . .

"Great," I allowed. "But why would Harold do something like that, and why would you two go along with it?"

"Like I said, we've all been friends for a long time, and he asked us to do it as a favor. Said he forgot to ask you a question before they took you away, and he didn't want to ask it when any of the cops might be listening in."

"I thought conversations between attorneys and clients were supposed to be private."

"Sometimes what's supposed to be doesn't match up with what is," Roger replied somberly.

"What's the question?"

"Do you have a cleaning lady?"

I could see that in focusing on the employees of the restaurant, I had forgotten the one person who had total access to my home once a week, usually when I was downstairs working. Marina would show up early in the day, wrestling her vacuum cleaner and cleaning supplies up the stairs. When she finished, my apartment would be spotless. She would pick up the hundred dollar bill I usually left for her on the dining room table and disappear, sometimes without my having even laid eyes on her. But the idea that Marina would be spying on me or going through my files? That was ridiculous. For one thing, she barely speaks English.

"Yes," I answered. "Yes, I do."

"What's her name?"

"Marina Ochoa."

"Where does she live?"

"In Glendale somewhere."

"You don't have her address?"

"No, I don't. I pay her in cash. There's never been any paperwork."

"No references, no nothing?" my interrogator asked.

"Look," I said, "my other cleaning lady quit several months ago. I was getting ready to place an ad for another one when Marina showed up asking for a job cleaning the bar and the restaurant. She spoke so little English that I had to have one of the dishwashers interpret for us. I explained that I have a commercial company that comes in to do the heavy cleaning in both the bar and the restaurant.

"When I told her that, she looked absolutely crushed and burst into tears—she was that desperate to find a job. Turns out she's a single mom supporting two little kids, ages five and three. I couldn't help but feel sorry for her, and with her right there, ready and willing to work, I was happy to dodge the agony of having to place an ad and interview people. I asked her if she'd consider cleaning my apartment and hired her on the spot. She's been cleaning my place ever since and doing a great job of it."

"Tears," Roger muttered. "They'll sucker a poor guy every single time. How long has she worked for you?"

"Three months now, maybe. She started toward the end of August."

"What days?"

"Sometimes on Fridays, sometimes on Thursdays, depending on her kids' schedules. It doesn't matter to me which day as long as she comes once a week. And like I said, she leaves the place spotless."

"Who lets her in and out?"

That's when I realized Roger wasn't just an old duffer—he was a smart old duffer, too, just like his pal Harold.

"You were a cop, weren't you?" I said.

He grinned. "Used to be," he said, "homicide, but that was a long time ago. Harold and me used to be on opposite sides of the fence. He won more times than I thought he should have. I always suspected that he cheated, and now I know that for sure. These days, though, when someone needs a hand, we usually work together."

"To help me?"

"Hell, I barely know who you are, you little whippersnapper. To help Tim, of course. Us old law enforcement types have to stick together—cops, attorneys, judges—you name it. The older you get, the less those old divisions matter. When somebody runs up the flag, we're all there, Johnny-on-the-spot. So stop stalling and answer the question. Who lets your undocumented alien cleaning lady in and out of your apartment?"

"She parks out behind the restaurant, comes in through the kitchen, and goes up the stairs."

"Is the upstairs door locked or unlocked?"

"Usually it's unlocked. Look," I added, sounding exasperated, "I'm right there the whole time."

Roger replied by asking yet another question. "Does Marina have a cell phone?"

"Probably, but I don't have the number. No point in my calling her. I don't speak Spanish."

"Which day did she come do the cleaning for the past several weeks?"

"She was there on Thursday this past week. I'm not sure about the others."

"You got surveillance cameras?"

"You bet. Top of the line. They cover the front door, the back door, and both parking lots. There are also cameras over the bar and over the cash register in the dining room."

"How long do you keep the files?"

"They go to my security company. As far as I know, they keep them indefinitely. After all, they're just computer files. It's not like the old days when there were miles of physical tapes taking up space."

"Which security company?"

I gave him the name. If I'd had either my phone or my computer with my address book in it, I could have given him the phone number and the account number. Sitting in a jail cell, I didn't have access to either one.

A new jailer came down the hallway. "All right, Mr. Holmes and Mr. Palmer. Someone has posted your bail. Can the two of you leave together, or do I need to take you out separately?"

"Don't bother," Roger said. "We'll be fine, won't we, Matt? We've cooled our heels long enough to bury the hatchet."

A pretend hatchet, I thought, as the two old codgers were led away to report their findings to their pal and mine, Harold Meeks. Once they left, I fell asleep—on the metal bench, with no pillow necessary. They woke me up at what the clock in an office outside the cell block said was three and led me into a courtroom in the building across the way to be arraigned. I pleaded innocent, of course, and then came the bail hearing.

Even though I could see Harold was tiring, he stood up, leaning on his walker, and made a good case for my being allowed out on bail. He told them I was an up-standing citizen with close ties to the community. He insisted that since my vehicle had been hauled away to the impound lot by the CSI investigators and since my passport had been confiscated as well, I was in no danger of fleeing the area to avoid prosecution. The upshot was, I was allowed to post a $500,000 bond, courtesy of Tim O'Malley. After that, they let me change clothes and gave me back my goods.

When it came time to leave the building, I walked out expecting to have to call for a cab. (Where's a decent pay phone when you need one?) Instead, I found a spit-and-polished venerable old Lincoln Town Car complete with a uniformed driver waiting out front. The driver got out of the vehicle and hurried to meet me.

"Mr. Dixon?"

I nodded.

"This way, please."

When he opened the back door for me, I slid onto the backseat and found Harold sitting slumped next to the far window. Out of sight of the detectives and the judge, he seemed to have shrunk. When he glanced at his watch, I followed suit and looked at mine, too. It was four-fifteen.

"Way past my bedtime," he announced. "Let's get me back to your place. I need my beauty sleep."

In other words, I still had an overnight guest.

"By the way," he added, "when we get back to the Roundhouse, your people are going to be full of questions. You can't afford to talk to them anymore than you can afford to talk to the cops. I've got operatives looking into the Marina Ochoa situation, but we can't risk taking any of your other employees off the list of suspects just yet. If they ask, tell them you've been advised not to discuss it."

"Yes, sir," I said. "Will do."

In less than twenty-four hours of dealing with Harold Meeks, he had made a believer of me, right along with that search warrant crew he had held at bay on the stairway outside my apartment.

It turns out he was right to have warned me to keep quiet. The people at the Roundhouse greeted us as though we were the second coming with cheers, hugs, handshakes, and tears all around. I helped Harold up the stairs and into the guest room. When I turned around, expecting to go back down to fetch his walker, I discovered Matty had beaten me to the punch and brought it upstairs.

"It was on the noon news," she said. "They're saying you murdered your ex-wife. I didn't even know you had an ex-wife."

"That's because it's not something I like to discuss. And my attorney—Harold here," I said, gesturing over my shoulder toward the guest room, "says I'm not to talk about it now with anyone."

"Mum's the word, then," she said, giving me a second fierce hug. "All I can say about Mr. Meeks is bless his heart."

She left then. I went into the bedroom and showered. I needed to scrub the feel of that holding cell off my skin and out of my soul. No need to rub it out of my hair.

When I came back out to the living room, Charles Rickover had let himself in and made himself at home on the chintz sofa. He had somehow managed to talk his way around Matty and come upstairs with a cup of freshly brewed coffee in hand. Maybe I did need to keep my apartment door locked.

"What are you doing here?" I asked. "I thought you were going to Vegas."

"Did," he replied. "Flew there and back, chop-chop. You ever hear of the Wright brothers?"

"So what's up?"

"Katherine Melcher's husband—her most recent husband—is in the clear, at least as far as doing the deed himself. He was out of the country on business. I've got airline records, car rental receipts, and passport control stamps coming and going. He could have hired someone to do it, I suppose, but as far as I can tell, Katherine had landed herself a fat cat and was determined to hang onto this one. According to him, after ditching the drugs, she became really serious about working her program. That's when she changed her name from Faith to Katherine—when the two of them married. It was part of a joint effort on their part to put her past in the past. By the way, my reading on Melcher is that he really is heartbroken."

"The woman would have dumped him sooner or later, and cleaned him out, too, in the process," I said. "Knowing Faith the way I do, up close and personal, I suspect her husband probably just dodged a bullet."

"Speaking of husbands," Charles said. "I also checked on your old pal Rick Austin."

"What about him? Where's he?"

"Deceased. Katherine—she was still Faith back then—married him shortly after she left you. That was followed by a time when they both did a serious amount of coke. She ended up in rehab, cleaned up her act, and left him high and dry. Austin blew his brains out after she left."

Karma's a bitch. Much as I thought Rick deserved everything he got, I couldn't help having a moment of sympathy for the guy. After all, there but for the love of Grandma Hudson would go I.

"By the way," Charles said, "I managed to lay hands on the vic's telephone records."

"How did you do that?"

"Don't ask, don't tell. Harold can subpoena them later if he needs to, but it's always better to know what they're going to say before you do that. I've got the dates and times for all the calls that were placed from the pay phone downstairs. I've also got a record of the call to her cell phone that was placed from the swimming pool pay phone at the Talisman at 2:05 A.M.

"Katherine took the call. It lasted for over three minutes. Twenty minutes later she is seen on surveillance tapes leaving her building. That's the last record I've been able to find of her, although I've got someone in Vegas looking at the surveillance tapes of all the hotels along the Strip. Talk about looking for a needle in the haystack, but we have a little better idea of what we're looking for now. It'll turn up. As for the Talisman? What a dog of a hotel! They may have surveillance cameras hanging on ceilings all over the place, but that's just for show. The problem is, not one of them works."

"In other words, the surveillance tape that might have caught the killer and exonerated me doesn't exist?"

Charles nodded. "That's the way it looks. So, are you ready to take a ride?"

I wasn't so sure. My most recent experience with being given a ride hadn't turned out very well.

"Where to?"

"I want to show you something."

"Can't you just tell me?"

"Showing's better than telling. Come on."

Not particularly happy about it, I headed for the stairs. Out in the parking lot I was surprised to discover that Charles's ride was a fire-engine-red Corvette. Not brand new, but new enough to make a statement. The man may have hit bottom years earlier, when Tim O'Malley's daughter had walked out on him for another woman, but that had most likely been the beginning of a long upward path for which Pop O'Malley was most likely largely responsible. I wondered what Tim would think if I called him by that handle, too. Somehow I suspected that he wouldn't mind.

As Charles and I headed down Highway 60 and turned onto the 101, I was dying to ask where we were going, but I stifled. Both highways were clotted with late afternoon traffic. Inching along in the HOV lane, we drove across the near north end of the city—not the real north end because the city has now expanded northward far beyond where those traditional boundaries used to lay. On the far side of Scottsdale and still on the 101, we turned south, exiting toward downtown Scottsdale on East Chaparral, just north of Camelback. Charles turned left onto Scottsdale Road, drove past Goldwater, and pulled into a parking garage at Fashion Square. Instead of parking in a space on one of the lower levels, he drove all the way up to the roof and pulled into a spot at the far edge of the lot, looking north.

"What do you see?" he asked.

I looked at the mid-rise across the street. It obviously housed high-end condos. The spacious balconies were filled with plants in wildly colorful pots and furnished with equally high-end deck chairs and tables. The grounds around the base of the building were meticulously landscaped with towering palms, a carpet of lush green grass, and flower beds thick with recently planted petunias. Clearly this was a building where the residents weren't the least bit concerned about the high cost of water in the Valley of the Sun.

"It's a building," I said grumpily, annoyed at being

forced to play a guessing game. "Condos for the rich and famous."

"Rich and infamous maybe," Charles replied with a sly grin. "Who do you suppose lives here?"

"I have no idea."

"Your cleaning lady," he said. "Marina Ochoa. That's not the name she goes by here. Folks in the condo complex know her as Maria Fuentes, but believe me, this is where the woman known to you as Marina Ochoa lives. By the way, she doesn't have any kids. None at all."

I'm sure my jaw dropped. "You're kidding."

"Wish I was," Charles answered. "I got the license of her work car from the surveillance tapes at your security agency. That's an old Buick, and she doesn't park it here. She's got a sweet little SLK that she drives back and forth between Scottsdale and Peoria. The Buick is what she drives when she comes to see you. She keeps it parked, complete with her vacuum cleaner and tray of cleaning supplies stowed in the trunk, in a garage over in Peoria just a few blocks from the Roundhouse."

"I don't understand," I said. "How could she possibly afford to live here?"

"I'm sure her boyfriend pays the freight. Does the name Jeffrey Jones sound familiar?"

My jaw dropped again. Or maybe still. "She's hooked up with the hotel developer, the one who's trying to buy me out?"

"That's right. One and the same. I believe that's what Jones and Ochoa have been after this whole time—

they've been trying to get the goods on you for months now. Jones must have finally realized that he wouldn't be able to convince you to sell at what he wanted to pay, so he sent Marina to you along with her hard luck story in order to gain access to your private life. One or the other of them came up with the brilliant idea that if you were in jail facing homicide charges with the possibility of a long prison sentence, you might be more inclined to be reasonable."

"But I thought . . ."

"I know what you thought," Charles said. "You believed Marina's sob story about being an illegal immigrant and about her working her poor little fingers to the bone in order to support her poor fatherless children. Guess again. Her parents immigrated from Mexico long before she was born. She's a U.S. citizen with an honors degree in history and English from ASU. She went on to get an MBA from Thunderbird over in Glendale. That's where she and Jeffrey hooked up. He divorced his first wife—his starter wife—shortly thereafter."

"But she worked for me for months," I objected.

"True," Charles agreed, "and they must have been looking to make a huge score, considering she was willing to do that much hard physical labor just to have unlimited access to your private life. Believe me, the Maria Fuentes who lives here has a cleaning lady of her own. The really good news for us is that before she and Jeffrey became a couple, Maria spent several years working in the securities field. That means her fingerprints are on file. I'm hoping the criminalists dusting your file folders for prints will not only find hers, but they'll find them where we need them."

"Finding her prints won't mean anything," I objected. "She cleans my apartment. Her fingerprints are bound to be there."

"In your apartment maybe, but not on the file folders containing your private documents. I can't imagine you expected her to dust the file with your divorce decree in it on a regular basis."

"But what if she wore gloves?" I objected, thinking about the gloves Charles put on his hands before touching my computer keyboard.

"Crooks like these are arrogant," Charles said. "It won't ever have occurred to them that we're this smart. She's probably been snooping through your computer the whole time she's been working for you, looking for something they could use to bring you to heel. Then two things happened. First they found out that Faith Dixon had turned into Katherine Melcher who was living in Las Vegas. Then you decided to go to Vegas for that writing convention. What's it called again?"

"Bouchercon."

"Yes, Bouchercon. At that point they must have thought they hit the jackpot because it all seemed to fall into place. At some point along the way your sweet little Marina made a copy of your car keys—the trunk key anyway. I checked the tapes. The week of October fifteenth, the week Katy Melcher died, Marina cleaned your apartment on Thursday rather than Friday. I'm pretty sure she and Jeffrey drove to Vegas together the next day to scope out the situation. I'm sure they used the old Twelfth Step ruse to lure Katy out of the house at that hour of the morning. According to Katy's widower, she took late night calls from addicts trying to kick their drug and alcohol habits."

That was way more than I could get my head around. The idea of Faith or Katy or whoever she was going out on a late night mission of mercy and being murdered for it seemed utterly unlikely.

"What about the threatening phone calls?" I asked.

"They came on days when Marina Ochoa would have been working for you. They must have figured that would make your situation a slam dunk. Threatening calls come from the victim's ex before she's murdered? What could be better?"

"What about the e-mail from Deeny?" I asked.

"That's apparently legit," Charles said. "Because of the phone calls, Katy Melcher really was worried that you were coming after her."

"In other words, Marina and Jeffrey expected that the local cops would focus on me to the exclusion of anyone else."

"Exactly," Charles Rickover agreed. "It might have gone just that way had it not been for Pop. Without him, you would have been a goner. Had you decided to forgo a public defender in favor of hiring your own defense attorney, you would have been forced to sell the Roundhouse to the first available buyer just to cover legal fees. You'd be amazed to know how much a top flight homicide defense team costs these days."

Evening was settling in. Across the street, lights switched on in various units as people came home from work or whatever it was they did during the day.

"So what happens now?"

"The two cops from Las Vegas . . ." he paused.

"Detectives Jamison and Shandrow," I supplied.

"They may be a bit slow on the uptake, but they're not stupid. Bright and early tomorrow morning, I expect Harold will point them in the right direction. It may take a few weeks to straighten all this up, but sooner or later your name will be cleared, as though nothing ever happened, and Jeffrey and Maria Fuentes will be up in Vegas facing first degree murder charges—both murder and conspiracy to commit. They're the ones who are goners now."

Rickover reached down, turned the ignition, and the Corvette rumbled to life.

"Where to?" he asked. "Back home?"

"If you don't mind, I'd like to stop off in Sun City on the way. I need to see Tim O'Malley and tell him thank-you."

"Great," Charles said. "I was hoping you'd say that."

When Tim let us into his house that night, I shook his hand and said, "Thank you, Pop. It was the first time I ever called him that—the first but not the last.

"How on earth did you find all those guys?" I asked. "Harold, Roger, Matt, and even old Charlie here."

Charles Rickover and I had been through enough together that I thought my calling him Charlie was . . . well . . . long overdue.

Tim and Charlie both grinned. "You've heard of how cops used to be called the Thin Blue Line?" Tim asked.

I nodded.

"Our little group calls itself the Old Blue Line," Tim said. "Some of us are thinner than we ought to be and others are wider, but when one or the other of us has a problem and runs up the flag, we all come on the double."

"Thank you," I said again. "More than you know."

Pop served us iced tea and apologized that he'd already eaten his TV dinner and didn't have any food to offer. I said I knew a place where we could find some grub if we needed it.

Later, as we were leaving, Pop gripped my hand with both of his. "Aggie would be so happy about this," he said, "so very happy."

And I knew it to be true. Grandma Agatha Hudson would have been pleased as punch.

I took Charlie back to the Roundhouse and treated both of us to the biggest and best steaks we had in the kitchen. When I came upstairs, much later, there was no sound from the guest room and no sign of a light under the door, either. I tiptoed past, hoping not to disturb Harold Meeks. He had worked his tail off for me that day, and he deserved a good night's sleep.

It turns out, so did I. I crawled into bed and slept like a baby. It was ungodly early when I woke up the next morning. Staring at the clock, I saw it was 5:30 A.M. What had awakened me was the unaccustomed sound of people talking away in my apartment. Out in the main room I discovered Harold Meeks was up, dressed in his preferred courtroom attire, and chatting up an enthralled Matty, who had just brought his breakfast up from the kitchen—two fried eggs and a double helping of bacon along with his own pot of freshly brewed coffee.

"It's about time you showed up," Harold growled at me. "We've got places to go and things to do."

"I'll need to see if I can rent a car," I said. "I didn't have time to do that yesterday."

He shook his head as though dealing with a recalcitrant toddler. "I've got a driver and a limo," he said. "We'll take that. And when we leave here, I'd like you to bring along my two suitcases. By later this afternoon I think we'll have this little difficulty well in hand and I'll be able to go back home."

THE NEXT FEW days passed in a blur. Just as Charlie Rickover had predicted, once Harold pointed Jamison and Shandrow in the right direction, they ran with it. The woman named Marina Ochoa never came back to clean my apartment. She and Jeffrey Jones were arrested the following Wednesday. They fought extradition, but it didn't work, despite the fact that they had hired a high profile defense guy from California. It wasn't a surprise that Jeffrey suddenly had to liquidate his real estate holdings in order to pony up attorney's fees.

Life seemed to get back to normal at the Roundhouse Bar and Grill. I hired a new cleaning lady—the sister-in-law of one of my dishwashers. (No, Helena isn't an illegal, and her English is just fine, thank you very much.)

After jumping through all kinds of hoops, I finally got my Honda sedan back, and wished I hadn't. The bloody bat had been found in the trunk, almost in plain sight, but the CSIs had torn the whole interior of the car to pieces looking for trace evidence. The car was already old before that happened. When the insurance adjustor looked at it, he shook his head, said it was totaled, and gave me a check that was just enough to buy myself a slightly used Honda Gold Wing.

Shortly after that, a new batch of police officer recruits turned up at the police academy next door. One day a couple of weeks later my life changed forever when a little red-haired ball of fire named Joanna Brady—the newly minted Sheriff of Cochise County—marched into the Roundhouse, stepped up to my bar, and ordered herself a Diet Coke.

While attending the academy, she was also in the process of looking out for some poor guy from Douglas, a guy name Jorge, who was about to be given the shaft.

As soon as I met her, I was done for. She may have been a lot slower to come around, but as far as I was concerned, it was love at first sight. The fact that she went out on a limb to bail Jorge out of a pot of hot water didn't hurt things, either, at least not for me. Having recently been bailed out of my own pot of hot water, that was one thing about her that I really appreciated.

But what is it they say about once burned, twice shy? I had fallen head over heels once before, and I was determined that if Joanna was the one for me, I was going to take things slow and easy. I could see that she liked me—at least I thought she did—but that was about as far as things went before she finished up her academy training and went back home to Bisbee.

That's when my life took another unexpected turn. In the middle of December a guy named Clark Ashton showed up at the Roundhouse with an offer to buy me out. He had bought up all of Jeffrey Jones's properties as well as his permits and plans, and he was eager to get his new hotel building under way as soon as possible. We dickered back and forth for a time, but not that much, not that hard, and not that long, because Ashton wanted to buy, and by then I wanted to sell.

Bisbee's a little over two hundred miles to the southeast from Peoria. When you're head over heels in love, two hundred miles is entirely too much distance.

It took time for me to convince Joanna Brady that I was the new man in her life. She wasn't an easy sell. And I didn't tell her about someone trying to frame me for murder until much later in our relationship because I didn't want to spook her. It wasn't, in fact, until after Charlie called to let me know that Pop O'Malley had passed away in his sleep that I finally got up my nerve and told her the whole story once and for all.

"Tim O'Malley and his friends did all that?" she marveled once I had finished.

I nodded.

"And now I can't even meet the man long enough tell him thank-you?"

"No, I'm afraid you can't," I said, shaking my head. "Sorry."

"I'm sorry, too," she told me, wiping a tear from her eye. "He and your Grandma Hudson must have been quite a pair."

Thinking of the two of them together made me smile. "You're right," I said. "They certainly were."

Next from J. A. Jance

An old woman, a hoarder, is dying of emphysema
in Great Barrington, Massachusetts. While
cleaning out her house, her daughter, Liza
Machett, discovers a fortune in hundred dollar
bills hidden in the stacks of books and magazines.
Trying to discover the provenance of that money
will take Liza on a journey all the way to Joanna
Brady's Cochise County. In the meantime,
Joanna has problems of her own when a family
friend is found dead in a limestone cavern near
Bisbee. But are these seemingly unrelated cases
more closely connected than they appear?

Here is a sneak preview of

Remains of Innocence

Coming soon
from William Morrow
An Imprint of HarperCollins Publishers

Prologue

LIZA MACHETT'S HEART was filled with equal parts dread and fury as she pulled her beater Nissan into the rutted driveway of her mother's place, stopped, and then stepped out to stare at the weedy wasteland surrounding the crumbling farmhouse. In the eleven years since Liza had left home, the place that had once been regarded as messy or junky had become a scene of utter desolation.

Spring had come early to western Massachusetts and to the small plot of land outside Great Barrington that had been in her father's family for generations. Liza had heard that in a much earlier time, while her great-grandparents had lived there, both the house and the yard had been immaculate. People said Great-Grandma Machett herself had tended the garden full of prize winning roses that had surrounded the front porch. Shunning help from anyone, she had donned an old-fashioned homemade bonnet and spent hours toiling in the yard, mowing the grass with a push-powered mower.

Great-Grandma Machett had been gone for decades now, and so was all trace of her hard work and industry. Thickets of brambles and weeds had overrun the grass and choked out the roses. Long ago a swing had graced the front porch. Swinging on that with her much older brother, Guy, was one of Liza's few happy childhood memories. The swing was gone. All that remained of it were two rusty chains that dangled uselessly from eyebolts still screwed into the ceiling boards. As for the porch itself? It sagged in the middle, and the three wooden steps leading up to the front door were completely missing, making the door inaccessible.

As a consequence, Liza walked around the side of the house toward the back. On the way, she tried peering into the house through one of the grimy storm windows that had been left in place for years, but the interior view was obstructed by old-fashioned wooden window blinds that had been lowered to windowsill level and closed tight against the outside world. A shiver of understanding shot through Liza's body, even though the afternoon sun was warm on her skin. The blinds existed for two reasons: to keep prying eyes outside and to keep her mother's darkness inside. Liza was tempted to turn back, but she squared her shoulders and kept on walking.

In the backyard, the freestanding wood-framed one-car garage, set away from the house, had collapsed in on itself long ago, taking Selma's ancient Oldsmobile with it. That was the car Liza remembered riding in as a child—a late-1970s, two-toned cream-and-burgundy Cutlass that had once been her father's. Somewhere along the way, her mother had parked the Cutlass in the garage and told her children that the car quit working. Liza thought she had been in the third grade when her mother had announced that they no longer needed a car. From then on, Liza and Guy had been responsible for their own transportation needs—they could catch the bus, ride their bikes, or, worst case, walk. Now the vehicle was a rusted-out hulk with only a corner of the back bumper still visible through pieces of the splintered garage door. Looking at the wreckage, Liza wondered if her life would have been different had the car kept running. After all, that was about the same time her mother had turned into a recluse and stopped leaving the house.

The only outbuilding that seemed to be in any kind of reasonable repair was the outhouse. The well-trod footpath to it led through an otherwise impenetrable jungle of weeds and brambles. Liza had hated the outhouse growing up. The smell had been vile; the spiders that lurked in the corners and would swing down on cobwebs in front of her eyes had terrified her. The presence of the path told her that the anachronistic outhouse, probably one of the last ones in the county, was still in daily use. That made sense. The social worker had told her that Selma's electricity had been turned off months ago due to lack of payment. Without electricity to run the pump at the well, the house would no longer have any indoor plumbing, either.

Liza's father had left when she was a baby. She didn't

remember ever having met him, but she had heard stories about how, decades earlier, he and his father, working together, had remodeled the place for his widowed
grandmother, bringing the miracle of running water
and indoor toilets into the house. Legend had it Great-
Grandma Machett had stubbornly insisted on using the
outhouse and on keeping the hand pump at the kitchen
sink that drew water from a cistern near the house. If
that hand pump was, through some miracle, still in op-
eration, it was probably the only running water Liza's
mother had.

"Stubborn old bat," Liza muttered under her breath.

She had never admitted to the kids at school that they
used an outhouse at home. Guy hadn't told anyone about
that, either. Once Great-Grandma Machett passed on,
they had moved into her place, and after Liza's father left,
the only bathroom in the house had become Selma's private domain. No one else was allowed to use it because,
she had insisted, running all that water through the fau-
cets and down the toilet was a waste of electricity and a
waste of money.

"We're too poor to send money down the drain like
that," her mother had insisted. "I'm not going to waste
the pittance your no-good father left me on that."

That meant that the whole time Liza and Guy were in
grade school, they had been forced to do their sponge-
bath bathing at the kitchen sink. That was where they
had hand-washed their clothing as well. All that had been
doable until the hot water heater had given out, sometime
during Liza's last year of elementary school. After that it

had been cold water only, because heating water on top of the stove for baths or for washing clothes had been deemed another extravagant waste of electricity and money.

Liza remembered all too well the jeering boys on the grade-school playground who had bullied her, calling her "stinky" and "dirty." The stigma stayed with her. It was why, even now, she showered twice a day every day—once in the morning when she first got up, and again in the evening after she got home from work.

Gathering herself, Liza turned to face the back door of the house she hadn't stepped inside for more than a decade, even though the place where she lived now was, as the crow flies, less than five miles away. Looking up, she noticed that, in places, the moss-covered roof was completely devoid of shingles. Just last year, Olivia Dexter, her landlady in town, had replaced the roof over Liza's upstairs apartment in Great Barrington. That roof hadn't been nearly as bad as this one was, but Liza had seen firsthand the damage a leaky roof could do to ceilings and walls and insulation. How, she wondered, had her mother made it through the harsh New England winter weather with no electricity and barely any roof?

Liza's mission today was in her mother's kitchen, and that was where she would go. The disaster that inevitably awaited her in the rest of the house would have to be dealt with at a later time. She remembered all too well the narrow paths between towering stacks of newspapers and magazines that had filled the living room back when she was a girl. Maybe all those layers of paper had provided a modicum of insulation during the winters. Even so, Liza wasn't ready to deal with any of that now, not yet.

Liza made her way up the stairs and then stood for a moment with her hand on the doorknob, willing herself to find the courage to open it. She knew how bad the place had been eleven years earlier, on that distant morning when she had finally had enough and fled the house. Rather than facing it, she paused, unable to imagine how much worse it would be now and allowing a kaleidoscope of unwelcome recollections to flash in and out of focus.

The memory of leaving home that day was still vivid in her mind and heart, even all these years later. Her mother had stood on the front porch screaming taunts and insults at Liza as she had walked away, carrying all her worldly possessions in a single paper grocery bag. She had walked down the half-mile-long driveway with her eyes straight ahead and her back ramrod straight. There were still times, when she awakened in the middle of the night, that she could hear echoes of her mother's venomous shouts—*worthless slut, no-good liar, thief.* The ugly words had rained down steadily as she walked away until finally fading out of earshot.

Liza Machett had heard the old childhood rhyme often enough:

> *Sticks and stones may break my bones*
> *But words will never hurt me.*

That was a lie. Being called names did hurt, and the wounds left behind never really healed over. Liza's heart still bore the scars to prove it. She had learned through bitter experience that silence was the best way to deal with her mother's periodic outbursts. The problem was, silence went only so far in guaranteeing her safety. There were times when even maintaining a discreet silence hadn't been enough to protect Liza from her mother's seething anger.

Liza understood that, on that fateful day, a pummeling from her mother's fists would have come next had she not simply taken herself out of the equation. Their final confrontation had occurred just after sunrise on a warm day in May. It was the morning after Liza's high school graduation, an event that had gone totally unacknowledged as far as Selma Machett was concerned. Liza's mother, trapped in a debilitating web of ailments both real and imagined, hadn't bestirred herself to attend. When Liza had returned home late that night, dropped off by one of her classmates after attending a graduation party, Selma had been waiting up and had been beyond enraged when Liza came in a little after three. Selma had claimed that Liza had never told her about the party and that she'd been up all night frantic with worry and convinced that Liza had really been out "sleeping around."

For Liza, a girl who had never been out on a single date all through high school, that last insult had been the final straw. A few hours later, shortly after sunrise, Liza had quietly packed her bag to leave and had tiptoed to the door, hoping that her mother was still asleep. Unfortunately, Selma had been wide awake and still furious. She had hurled invectives after her departing daughter as

Liza walked across the front porch and down the steps. The porch had still had steps back then.

Liza walked briskly away with her head unbowed beneath Selma's barrage of insults. At the time, Liza's only consolation was that there were no neighbors nearby to witness her mother's final tirade. Walking away from the house, Liza had realized that she was literally following in her older brother's footsteps and doing the same thing Guy had done five years earlier. He too had walked away, taking only what he could carry, and he hadn't looked back.

Liza had been thirteen years old and in eighth grade on the day Guy left home for college. A friend had stopped by shortly after he graduated and given him a lift and a life. During the summer he had waited tables in the Poconos. Then, armed with a full-ride scholarship, he had enrolled at Harvard, which was only a little over a hundred miles away. As far as Liza was concerned, however, Harvard could just as well have been on another planet. Guy had never come back—not over Christmas that first year nor for any of the Christmases that followed, and not for summer vacations, either. From Harvard he had gone on to Maryland for medical school at Johns Hopkins. Unlike Guy, all Liza had to show for enduring years of her mother's torment was a high school diploma and a severe case of low self-esteem.

Did Liza resent her brother's seemingly charmed existence? You bet! It was perfectly understandable that he had turned his back on their mother. Who wouldn't? Liza remembered all too well the blazing battles between the two of them in the months and weeks before Guy left home. She also recalled her brother's departing words, flung over his shoulder as he walked out the door. "You're not my real mother."

Those words had been true for him, and that was his out—Selma was Guy's stepmother. Unfortunately, she was Liza's "real" mother. Half brother or not, however, Guy had always been Liza's big brother. In walking away from Selma, he had also walked away from Liza. He had left her alone to cope with a mentally damaged, self-centered woman who was incapable of loving or caring for anyone, including herself.

All the while Liza had been growing up, there had been no accounting for Selma's many difficulties, both mental and physical, real and imagined. There had been wild mood swings that most likely indicated Selma was bipolar—not that she'd ever gone to a doctor or a counselor to be given an official diagnosis. There had been episodes of paranoia in which Selma had spent days convinced that people from the government were spying on her. There was the time she had taken a pair of pliers to her own mouth and removed all the filled teeth because she was convinced the fillings were poisoning her. It wasn't until long after Liza left home that there was a name for the most visible of Selma's mental difficulties. She was a hoarder. Liza found it disquieting that hoarding was now something that could be spoken of aloud in polite company and that, in fact, there was even a reality television show devoted to the problem.

Liza had watched the show occasionally, with a weird

combination of horror and relief, but she had never found a way to say to any of the people who knew her now, "That was my life when I was growing up." Instead, like a voyeur driving past a terrible car wreck, she watched the various dysfunctional families on the small screen struggling with issues she knew intimately, from the inside out. In the well-ordered neatness of her own living room, she could compare what she remembered of her mother's house with the messes and horrors in other people's lives, all the while imagining what Selma's place must be like now after another decade of unchecked decline.

Sometimes what she saw on one of the shows moved her to tears. Occasionally the televised efforts of loved ones and therapists seemed to pay off and damaged people seemed to find ways to begin confronting what was wrong with their lives and perhaps make some necessary changes. With others, however, it was hopeless, and all the painful efforts came to naught. The people trying to help would throw things in the trash—broken toys, wrecked furniture, nonworking appliances—only to have the hoarder drag the garbage back into the house because it was too precious to be tossed out.

For her part, Liza suspected that Selma was one of the ones who wouldn't be helped or fixed. She doubted her mother would ever change, and Liza knew for a fact that she had neither the strength nor the will to force the issue. If Guy had offered to come home and help her? Maybe. But all on her own? No way.

As a teenager, Liza had dealt with the shame of how they lived—the grinding poverty and the utter filth of their existence—as best she could. She had put up with her mother's ever-declining health and occassional screaming rages. Liza's smallest efforts to clean anything up or throw away one of her mother's broken treasures had been met with increasingly violent outbursts on her mother's part. Liza understood now that she most likely wouldn't have survived high school had it not been for the timely intervention of first one and subsequently several of her teachers.

It had been at the end of phys ed during the first week of her freshman year. After class, some of the girls had been taunting Liza about being dirty when Miss Rose had come into the locker room unannounced and heard what they were saying. She had told Liza's tormentors to knock it off and had sent them packing. Ashamed to show her face, Liza had lingered behind, but when she came out of the locker room, Miss Rose had been waiting for her in the gym.

"How would you like a job?" she had asked.

"What do you mean, a job?" Liza had stammered.

"I need someone to come in after school each afternoon to wash and fold the towels," Miss Rose said. "I couldn't pay you much, say ten bucks a week or so, but you'd be able to shower by yourself and wash your own clothes along with the towels."

That was all Miss Rose ever said about it. Liza didn't know how Miss Rose had known so much about her situation. Maybe she had grown up in the same kind of squalor or with the same kind of mother. Not long after that, some of the coaches of the boys' sports teams had asked

Liza to handle their team laundry needs as well. Eventually she had been given her own key to both the gym and the laundry. She spent cold winter afternoons and hot spring days in the comforting damp warmth of the gym's laundry room, doing her homework, turning jumbles of dirty towels and uniforms into neat stacks and washing her own clothing at the same time. As for the money she earned? The collective fifty dollars a week she got for her efforts from various teachers and coaches, all of it paid in cash, was money that Liza's mother never knew about, and it made all the difference. It meant that Liza was able to eat breakfast and lunch in the school cafeteria rather than having to go hungry.

In the end, Liza had done the same thing her brother did—she left. But she didn't go nearly as far as her brother's hundred miles. Guy had been brilliant. Liza was not. Her mediocre grades weren't good enough for the kind of scholarship help that would have made college possible, but her work record with the coaches and teachers had counted as enough of a reference that she'd been able to land a job in Candy's, a local diner, the first week she was on her own. She had started out washing dishes and had worked her way up to waitress, hostess, and finally—for the last year—assistant manager. Candy had taught her enough about food handling that, in a pinch, she could serve as a passable short-order cook. She didn't earn a lot of money, but it was enough to make her self-supporting.

Liza's car was a ten-year-old rusted-out wreck of a Nissan, but it was paid for and it still ran. That was all she needed. Her home was a tiny upstairs apartment in an old house off Main Street in Great Barrington. It could be freezing cold in the winter and unbearably hot in the summer, as it was right now in this unseasonably late April heat wave, but the apartment was Liza's and Liza's alone, and she kept it immaculately clean.

She never left home in the morning without first washing and drying the dishes. Her bed was made as soon as she climbed out of it. Her dirty clothes went in a hamper, and when she came back from the Laundromat, her clean clothes went in dresser drawers or on hangers. Her floors were clean. Her trash always went out on time. There was never even so much as a hint of mouse droppings in the freshly laundered towels she took out of her tiny linen closet and held up to her face.

Driving out to her mother's place from the hospital that morning, Liza had measured the distance on the odometer. She had been surprised to realize that the hospital was a mere four miles and her apartment only another mile beyond that from her mother's squalid farmhouse. Somehow, in all the intervening years, she had imagined the distance to be much greater. She had always told herself that she would never go back, no matter what, and she hadn't—not until today. Not until a social worker had tracked her down at work and given her the bad news.

Selma had evidently fallen. Unable to get up, she hadn't been found for a number of days. A postman had finally notified someone that her mail was piling up in the mailbox at the end of the driveway, and a uniformed deputy had been dispatched to do a welfare check. Selma had been found unconscious on the floor of a room that bore no resemblance to a living room. Revived at the scene, she had been forcibly removed from her house and taken by ambulance to the hospital. Selma was currently in the ICU where doctors were doing their best to rehydrate her with IV fluids and nourishment. Liza had been told that Selma was in stable condition, but the social worker had made it plain that the outlook wasn't good. Despite her relatively young age—Selma was only fifty-seven—her emphysema was much worse, and her next stop would most likely be a bed in the hospice care unit of the Sunset Nursing Home. The end might come in as little as a few days or a few weeks at the most.

Hearing the news, Liza tried to feel sorry for her mother, but she could not. The woman had brought it on through years of chain-smoking and neglecting her health. Liza had always told herself that as far as her mother was concerned, she was done; that if Selma ever needed help, Liza wouldn't go—wouldn't cross the street or lift a finger to help her mother, but when push came to shove, Liza had caved.

The social worker had come by the diner to let Liza know. Before the social worker had finished telling her what had happened, Liza had her phone in hand and was dialing her boss's home number to let Candy know that she was going to need someone else to cover her shifts for the next few days. Within forty-five minutes, she had turned up at the ICU, as dutiful as any loving daughter. She rushed down the polished corridor to Selma's room as though there hadn't been a lifetime's worth of bad history and eleven years of total estrangement between them.

And what had Liza expected for her trouble? Maybe she hoped the long-delayed reunion with her mother would turn into one of those schmaltzy Hallmark moments, with Selma reaching out to embrace her daughter and saying how precious Liza was; how much she had missed her; how glad she was to see her; how sorry she was for all the awful things she had said those many years ago. Of course, that wasn't what happened—not at all.

Selma Machett's eyes had popped open when Liza warily approached her mother's bedside.

"Where've you been?" Selma demanded. "What took you so long? I told them not to do it, but those stupid jerks in the ambulance brought me here anyway. And when I told them I needed my cookbook, they couldn't be bothered. You know the one I mean—my old *Joy of Cooking*. I need it right now. I want you to go to the house and get it—you and nobody else."

No, not a Hallmark moment by any means. Liza understood full well that her mother simply issued orders rather than making requests. *Please* and *Thank you* weren't part of Selma's vocabulary. Liza also knew that her mother had a vast collection of cookbooks, moldering in her filthy kitchen. Not that she'd ever used any of them. In fact, Liza couldn't remember her mother ever cooking a single meal. All the while Liza was growing up, they'd survived on take-out food, burgers and pizza that her mother had somehow managed to pay for. Afterward, the wrappers and boxes, sometimes with stray pieces of pizza still inside, were left to rot where they fell.

Even though Liza knew it to be a futile exercise, she attempted to reason with her mother. "Look, Mom," she said placatingly. "They have a very good kitchen here at the hospital. You don't need a cookbook. When it's time for you to eat, they'll bring your food on a tray."

"I don't care about that," Selma snapped. "I want my cookbook, and I want it now. The key's still where it's always been, under the mat on the back porch. Go now. Be quick about it."

Which is exactly how Liza came to be here. When she lifted the mat, it disintegrated in her hands, falling in a brittle heap of disconnected rubbery links on the top step. After inserting the key and turning it in the lock, Liza stood on the far side of the door for the better part of five minutes, trying to summon the courage to venture inside.

Knowing that the power was off and that the inside of the house would be beyond filthy, Liza had done what she could to come prepared. She had stowed a small jar of Vicks in her purse. She had stopped at the drugstore and bought a package of face masks and a box of surgical gloves. Finally, after dabbing the eye-watering salve under her nostrils and donning both a mask and a pair of gloves, she opened the door.

No amount of advance warning could have prepared her. The stench was unimaginable. Covering her face with her hand, Liza fell backward and fought, unsuccessfully, to push down the bile that rose in her throat. Giving up, she clung to the crooked porch rail and heaved the hamburger she had eaten for lunch into a waist-high mound of moldering trash that had accumulated next to the steps.

At last, wiping her mouth on the tail of her blouse and steeling herself for another assault on her senses, Liza edged the door open again. To begin with, that was all she could do—crack it open. A heaping wall of rotting garbage, this one stacked almost ceiling high, kept the door from swinging open completely. As Liza sidled into the room, finger-sized roaches and fist-sized spiders scurried for cover.

Selma had always been a chain-smoker. Underlying everything else was the stench of decades'worth of unfiltered Camels, but that was only in the background. In the foreground were the unmistakable odors of rotting garbage and of death. Liza chalked up the latter to some dead varmint—a rat or mouse perhaps—or maybe a whole crew of them whose decaying corpses were buried somewhere under the mounds of trash.

Leaving the back door open, Liza stepped gingerly into the room, sticking to a narrow path that meandered through the almost unrecognizable kitchen between unstable cliffs of what looked to her like nothing but refuse. The mountains of garbage were tall enough that they obscured the windows, leaving the room in a hazy gloom. Although Liza knew this to be the kitchen, there was no longer any sign of either a stove or a sink. If her great-grandmother's hand pump still existed, it was invisible, completely buried under masses of debris. The refrigerator was hidden behind another evil-smelling mound.

Standing on tiptoe, Liza saw that the door to the freezer compartment was propped open, revealing a collection of long-abandoned contents, their labels indecipherable behind a thick layer of mold. Next to the fridge was the tall stand-alone bookcase that held her mother's cookbooks. She could see the books, their titles completely obscured behind a thick curtain of undisturbed spiderwebs.

There were few things in life that Liza hated more than spiders and their sticky webs. These were clotted with the desiccated corpses of countless insects who had mistakenly ventured into the forest of silky threads and died for their trouble. Liza knew that hidden behind the layer of webs was the book she was charged with retrieving. If she squinted, she could almost make out the bright red letters of the title through the scrim of fibers.

Gritting her teeth, Liza pushed the webs aside far enough to reach the book. She had the cover in her hand when a spider glided down a web and landed on her arm. Screaming and leaping backward, Liza dropped the book and, with a desperate whack from the back of her hand, sent the startled spider sailing across the room. When Liza looked down, she saw that the book had landed spine up on the floor, sitting like a little tent pitched on the dirty floor among an accumulation of mouse turds. And scattered across the filthy floor around the half-opened book were what appeared to be five one-hundred-dollar bills.

For a moment, Liza could barely believe what she was seeing. Squatting down, she picked them up one at a time. The unaccustomed gloves on her hands made for clumsy fingers, and it didn't help that her hands were shaking. She examined the bills. They looked real enough, but where had they come from, and what were they doing in Selma's copy of *Joy of Cooking*?

Stuffing the bills in the pocket of her jeans, Liza picked up the book itself. Holding it by the spine, she flapped the pages in the air. As she did so, two more bills fluttered out from between the pages and drifted to the floor.

Liza was amazed. Seven hundred dollars had been hidden in one of her mother's cookbooks! Where had the money come from? How long had it been there? Had her mother kept the bills squirreled away the whole time Liza had been growing up—the whole time she was struggling to fit in at school while wearing thrift shop clothing and buying her school lunches with money she had earned by doing sports teams' laundry? Had there been money hiding in her mother's cookbook even then? And if there were seven hundred dollars in this one book, what about the others? Was money concealed in those as well?

Using the book in her hand, Liza swept away the remaining spiderwebs and reached for another book. The two mammoth volumes next to the empty spot left behind by the absent *Joy* turned out to be Julia Child's *Mastering the Art of French Cooking*, Volumes 1 and 2. A quick shuffle through the 652 pages of Volume 1 was good for five hundred bucks. Ditto for Volume 2. With close to two thousand dollars now crammed in her pocket, Liza reached for the next book on the shelf: *Betty Crocker's Quick and Easy*. A thorough examination of that one surfaced only three hundred dollars, but by the time Liza had worked her way through the entire collection, she had amassed close to thirty thousand dollars. It was more money in one place than Liza had ever seen in her life, more money than she had ever thought her mother had to her name.

At last the bookshelf was cleared. The cookbooks, plucked clean of their hidden treasure, lay in a careless heap on the floor. During the search, Liza had gone from first being surprised and amazed to being beyond furious. The more money she found, the more she wondered if the small fortune in hidden bills had been in Selma's possession the whole time. If so, why had Selma always pretended to be poor? Why had she denied her children and herself simple creature comforts like running water and hot baths that some of that money might have afforded all of them?

As a teenager, Liza had never thought to question the fact that they were poor. Their poverty was an all too demonstrable reality. She had listened in silence while her mother bewailed their fate, complaining about their lot and blaming the fact that Liza's father had run off—presumably with another woman—leaving them with barely a roof over their heads and not much else. Liza knew from something her brother had said that before Anson Machett bailed, he'd at least had the decency to quitclaim the family home—the farm and the run-down house that had belonged to his great-grandparents—to his soon-to-be-abandoned wife. Before Guy left home, Selma had told the kids that their father was dead, having died in a car wreck somewhere in California. Selma had offered no details about a memorial service or a funeral. First their father was gone and then he was dead.

Now, at age twenty-nine and standing in the desolation of Selma's filthy kitchen, Liza Machett found herself asking for the very first time if anything her mother had told them was true. If Selma had lied to them about being poor, maybe she had lied about everything else, too.

After gathering the last of the money from the books, Liza stayed in the kitchen for a long time, too stunned to know what to do next. Should she go to the hospital and confront her mother about all this? Should she demand to be told the truth, once and for all?

Ultimately Liza realized that a direct confrontation would never work. Instead, she reached down, pawed through the pile of books, and retrieved the one at the bottom of the heap—the *Joy of Cooking.* Pulling the thick wad of bills from her pocket, she extracted seven of them and placed them in various spots throughout the book. If Selma remembered the exact pages where she had stuck the money, then Liza was screwed. Otherwise, Liza could hand the book over to Selma and act as though she hadn't a clue that there was money hidden inside.

She hoped the trick would work. If Selma didn't realize Liza had discovered her secret, it would buy Liza time—time to look for answers on her own and to sift through the rest of the debris in the house. Liza knew that once she reached the living room, she would find stacks of back issues of *National Geographic, Life,* and *Reader's Digest* as well. What if those had all been seeded with money in the same way the cookbooks had? There was only one way to find out for sure, and Liza was determined to do so—she intended to search through every single one.

Back outside with the cookbook in hand, Liza stripped off her mask and gloves and drew in a deep breath of clean fresh air. Her Nissan, parked at the end of the driveway, sat unlocked and with the windows wide open. Leaving the windows open kept the interior from getting too hot. That was important especially during hot weather since the Nissan's AC had stopped working long ago.

Liza dropped the book on the passenger seat before going around to the other side to climb in. When she turned to fasten her seat belt, the tail end of her pony-tail swished in front of her face. That's when she smelled it—the same pungent combination of foul odors that had plagued her as a girl and that had been the cause of so much painful bullying from other kids. The odor of decay in her mother's home had somehow permeated Liza's hair and clothing. She could barely tolerate sitting in the car knowing that she was probably leaving the same stinky residue on the car seats and carpeting.

Hating the very idea, Liza headed for her apartment rather than for the hospital. She would go see her mother and deliver the book, but only after she had showered and washed her hair. Looking at the book, she realized it probably smelled the same way. Once she hit Great Barrington, she pulled in to the drive-in window of the local Dunkin' Donuts and ordered a bag of their Breakfast Blend coffee beans. She had heard that coffee beans helped get rid of bad smells. It seemed worth a try.

At home, Liza located a gallon-size Ziploc bag. She placed the book inside that along with all the bills she had stuffed in her pockets. Then, having added the whole beans, she zipped the bag shut before going into the bathroom to shower.

She stood under the stream of hot water for the next fifteen minutes, trying to wash away the dirt and grit from her mother's house. With her eyes closed, she hoped she was washing off something else as well—the soul-destroying contamination of her mother's many betrayals.

She needed to send Selma Machett's perfidy circling down the drain every bit as much as she needed to rid herself of the odor of mouse droppings and rotting food that, despite all her scrubbing, still seemed to cling to her skin.

Chapter 1

THE SUN WAS just coming up over the distant Chiricahua Mountains to the east of High Lonesome Ranch when a rooster crowed at ten past five in the morning. At that hour of the day, it might have been one of the ranch's live resident roosters announcing the arrival of a new day, but it wasn't. This was the obnoxiously distinctive crowing of Sheriff Joanna Brady's cell phone.

Groping for the device in its charging stand on the bedside table, Joanna silenced the racket and glanced across the bed. Her husband, Butch, slept undisturbed with a pillow pulled over his head. Taking the phone in hand, Joanna scrambled out of bed. Now that Lady, her rescued Australian shepherd, had decamped to a spot next to Joanna's son's bed, she no longer had to deal with tripping over a dead-to-the-world dog when it came to late-night callouts, which usually meant there was serious trouble somewhere in Cochise County.

Hurrying into the bathroom and closing the door behind her, Joanna answered, "Sheriff Brady."

"Chief Bernard here," a male voice rumbled in her ear. "Sorry to wake you at this ungodly hour, but I could sure use your K-9 unit if you can spare them."

Alvin Bernard was the police chief in Bisbee, Arizona. Once known as a major copper-producing town, Bisbee's current claim to fame was its reputation as an arts colony. It was also the county seat. Alvin Bernard's departmental jurisdiction ended at Bisbee's city limits, the line where Joanna's countywide jurisdiction began.

Years earlier, Joanna had been elected to the office of sheriff in the aftermath of her first husband's death. Andy Brady had been running for the office when he died in a hail of bullets from a drug cartel's hit man. When Joanna was elected sheriff in her late husband's stead, members of the local law enforcement old boys' network had sneered at the outcome, regarding her election as a straight-up sympathy vote, and had expected Joanna to be sheriff in name only. She had surprised the naysayers by transforming herself into a professional police officer. As she developed a reputation for being a good cop, that initial distrust had melted away. She now had a cordial working relationship with most of her fellow police administrators, including Bisbee's Chief Bernard.

"What's up?"

"Junior Dowdle's gone missing from his folks' house up the canyon. He left his room sometime overnight by climbing out through a bedroom window. His bed hasn't been slept in. Daisy's frantic. She and Moe have been up and down the canyon several times looking for him. So far there's no trace."

Junior, Moe and Daisy Maxwell's developmentally disabled foster son, had been found abandoned by his paid caregiver at a local arts fair several years earlier. Once his blood relatives were located, they had declined to take him back. That was when the Maxwells had stepped in. They had gone to court and been appointed his legal guardians. Since then they had cared for Junior as their own, giving him purpose in life by teaching him to work as a combination busboy and greeter in the local diner that bore Daisy's name.

In recent months, though, Junior's behavior had become increasingly erratic, both at home and in the restaurant. Only a few weeks earlier the family had been given the dreaded but not-so-surprising diagnosis—not so surprising because the doctor had warned the Maxwells a year earlier about the possibility. Now in his early sixties, Junior was suffering from a form of dementia, most likely Alzheimer's, an affliction that often preyed on the developmentally disabled. Under most circumstances, a missing person report of an adult wouldn't have merited an immediate all-out response. Because Junior was considered to be at risk, however, all bets were off.

"He's on foot then?" Joanna asked.

"Unless some Good Samaritan picked him up and gave him a ride," Alvin answered.

"Okay," Joanna said. "I'll give Terry a call and see what, if anything, he and Spike can do about this."

Terry Gregovich was the human half of Joanna's departmental K-9 unit. Spike, a seven-year-old German shepherd, was Terry's aging canine partner.

"You're sure Junior left through a window?"

"Daisy told me they've been concerned about Junior maybe wandering off, so they've gotten into the habit of keeping both the front and back doors to the house deadbolted. It was warm overnight, so Daisy left the window cracked open when Junior went to bed. Had Daisy Maxwell ever raised a teenage son, she would have known she needed to lock the window as well."

"That's how he got out?"

"Yup, it looks like Junior raised the window the rest of the way, pushed open the screen, and climbed out."

"Do you want me to see if I have any additional patrol officers in the neighborhood who could assist with the search?"

"That would be a huge favor," Alvin said. "We'll be using the parking lot of St. Dominick's as a center of operations. Once the neighbors hear about this, there will be plenty of folks willing to help out. From my point of view, the more boots we have on the ground, the better. It'll make our lives easier if Terry and Spike can point the search crews in the right direction."

"I'll have Dispatch get back to you and let you know if anyone else is available."

She called Terry first, dragging him out of bed, then she called Dispatch to let Tica Romero, her overnight dispatcher, know what was going on. The City of Bisbee and Cochise County had a standing mutual aid agreement in place, but it was better to have everything officially documented in case something went haywire. Mutual aid in the course of a hot pursuit was one matter. For anything else, Joanna had to be sure all the necessary chain-of-command *t*'s were crossed and *i*'s were dotted.

Butch came and went through the bathroom while Joanna was in the shower. Once dried off, she got dressed, donning a neatly pressed everyday khaki uniform and a lightweight pair of lace-up hiking boots. Early on in her career as sheriff, she had worn business-style clothing, most of which couldn't accommodate the Kevlar vest she wore each day right along with her other officers. Then there was the matter of footwear. After going through countless pairs of pantyhose and wrecked pairs of high heels, she had finally conceded defeat, putting practicality ahead of fashion.

Minutes later, with her bright red hair blown dry and her minimally applied makeup in place, she hurried out to the kitchen, where she found Butch brewing coffee and unloading the dishwasher.

"What's up?" he asked.

"I'm on my way to St. Dominick's," she explained. "Junior Dowdle took off sometime overnight. Alvin Bernard is using the parking lot at St. Dom's as a center of operations, and he's asked for help from my K-9 unit."

Joanna knew that her husband maintained a personal interest in Junior's life and welfare. She and Butch hadn't been married when Junior came first to Bisbee after being abandoned at the Arts and Crafts Fair in Saint David. Bringing him to Bisbee in her patrol car, Joanna had been stumped about where to take him. Her own home was out. The poor man wasn't a criminal and he wasn't ill. That meant that neither the jail nor the hospital were possibilities, either. In the end, she had taken him to Butch's house in Bisbee's Saginaw neighborhood, where Junior had stayed for several weeks. A restaurant Butch had owned previously, the Roundhouse in Peoria, Arizona, had once fielded a Special Olympics team, and Butch had been one of the team coaches. He had taken charge of Junior with practiced grace and had kept him until more suitable permanent arrangements could be made with the Maxwells.

"You're going to join the search?" Butch asked, handing Joanna a cup of coffee.

She nodded.

"All right," he said. "If they haven't found Junior by the time I drop the kids off at school, I'll stop by and help, too. Do you want breakfast before you head out? It won't take more than a couple of minutes to fry eggs and make toast."

That was one of the advantages of marrying a man who had started out in life as a short-order cook. Joanna didn't have to think long before making up her mind. Depending on how her day went, the next opportunity to eat might be hours away. Besides, this was Alvin's case. She and her people were there as backup only. In addition, Butch's over-easy eggs were always perfection itself.

"Sounds good," she said. "Do you want any help?"

"I'm a man on a mission," Butch told her with a grin. "Sit down, drink your coffee, and stay out of the way."

Doing as she'd been told, Joanna slipped into the breakfast nook. She'd taken only a single sip of coffee when Dennis, their early-bird three-year-old, wandered into the kitchen dragging along both his favorite blankie and his favorite book—*The Cat in the Hat*. There wasn't a person in the household who didn't know the story by heart, but Joanna pulled him into a cuddle and started reading aloud, letting him turn the pages.

They were halfway through the story when two dogs scrambled into the kitchen—Jenny's stone-deaf black lab, Lucky, and a relatively new addition to their family, a fourteen-week-old golden retriever puppy named Desi. The puppy carried the tattered remains of one of Jenny's tennis shoes in his mouth. Both dogs dove for cover under the table of the breakfast nook as an exasperated Jenny, wearing a bathrobe and with her wet hair wrapped in a towel, appeared in the doorway.

"I was only in the shower for five minutes," she fumed. "That's all it took for Desi to wreck my shoe."

"Wait until you have kids of your own," Butch warned her. "Desi will be over it a lot faster than a baby will. Besides, it could have been worse. It's only a tennis shoe. When Lucky was a pup, he always grabbed one of your boots."

Leveling a sour look in Butch's direction, Jenny knelt down by the table. Rather than verbally scolding the miscreant puppy, she glowered at him and gave him two-thumbs down—her improvised sign language equivalent of "bad dog." Next she motioned toward her body with one hand, which meant "come." Finally she held out one cupped hand and patted the cupped one with her other hand, the hand signal for "give it to me."

There was a momentary pause under the table before Desi squirmed out from under his temporary shelter and handed over the mangled shoe. In response, Jenny gave him a single thumb-up for "good dog." Two thumbs would have meant "very good dog," and currently, no matter what he did right, Desi didn't qualify. Once the puppy had been somewhat forgiven, Lucky dared venture out, too. He was rewarded with the two-thumb treatment before Jenny took her damaged shoe in hand and left the room with both dogs on her heels.

Joanna couldn't help but marvel at how the hand signals Jenny had devised to communicate with Lucky were now making it possible for her to train a service dog as part of a 4-H project. There was the expectation that, at some time in the future, Desi would make a difference in some person's life by serving as a hearing assistance dog.

"Your breakfast is on the table in five," Butch called after Jenny as she left the room. "Two eggs scrambled, whole wheat toast. Don't be late."

"I'm afraid training that dog is more work than Jenny anticipated," Joanna commented. "After losing Tigger the way we did, I'm worried about her ability to let Desi go when it's time for him to move on." Tigger, their previous dog, a half golden retriever, half pit bull mix, had succumbed within weeks of being diagnosed with Valley Fever, a fungal disorder commonly found in the desert Southwest that often proved fatal to dogs.

"Jenny and I have already discussed that," Butch said,

"but you're right. Talking about letting go of a dog is one thing. Handing the leash over to someone else is another."

Joanna nodded in agreement. "We all know that when it comes to horses and dogs, Jennifer Ann Brady has a very soft heart."

"Better horses and dogs than boys," Butch observed with a grin. "Way better."

That was a point on which Joanna and Butch were in complete agreement.

"Speaking of horses, did she already feed them?"

For years the horse population on High Lonesome Ranch had been limited to one—Kiddo, Jenny's sorrel gelding, who was also her barrel-racing partner. Recently they had added a second horse to the mix, an aging, blind Appaloosa mare that had been found, starving and dehydrated, in the corral of a recently foreclosed ranchette near Arizona Sunsites. The previous owners had simply packed up and left town, abandoning the horse to fend for herself. When a neighbor reported the situation, Joanna had dispatched one of her Animal Control officers to retrieve the animal.

After a round of veterinary treatment at county expense, Butch and Jenny had trailered the mare home to High Lonesome, where she seemed to have settled into what were supposedly temporary digs in the barn and corral, taking cues on her new surroundings from Kiddo while she gained weight and recovered. Dennis, after taking one look at the horse, had promptly dubbed her Spot.

In Joanna's opinion, Spot was a far better name for a

dog than it was for a horse, but Spot she was, and Spot she remained. Currently inquiries were being made to find Spot a permanent home, but Joanna suspected that she had already found one. When Butch teased Joanna by saying she had turned High Lonesome Ranch into an unofficial extension of Cochise County Animal Control, it was more true than not. Most of the dogs that had come through their lives had been rescues, along with any number of cast-off Easter bunnies and Easter chicks. Now, having taken in a hearing impaired dog and a visually impaired horse, they were evidently a haven for stray animals with disabilities as well.

"The horses are fed," Butch answered. "Jenny and the dogs went out to do that while I was starting the coffee and you were in the shower."

By the time Jenny and the now more subdued dogs returned to the kitchen, Joanna was ready to head out. After delivering quick good-bye kisses all around, she went to the laundry room to retrieve and don her weapons. For Mother's Day a few weeks earlier, Butch had installed a thumb recognition gun safe just inside the door. Located below a light switch, it was within easy reach for Joanna's vertically challenged five-foot-four frame. With her two Glocks safely stowed—one in a holster on her belt and the other, her backup weapon, in a bra-style holster—Sheriff Joanna Brady was ready to face her day.

It generally took the better part of ten minutes for Joanna to drive her county-owned Yukon the three miles of combination dirt and paved roads between High Lonesome Ranch at the base of the Mule Mountains and her office at the Cochise County Justice Center. In this instance she drove straight past her office on Highway 80 and headed into Bisbee proper. St. Dominick's Church, up the canyon in Old Bisbee, was another four miles beyond that.

The time Joanna spent in her car each day gave her a buffer between her job and her busy home life. On this late-spring day, she spent some of the trip gazing off across the wide expanse of the Sulphur Springs Valley, taking in the scenery—the alternating squares of cultivated fields and tracts of wild desert terrain punctuated with mesquite trees—that stretched from the nearby Mule Mountains to the Chiricahua Mountains in the distance, some thirty miles away. She loved the varying shades of green that springtime brought to the desert, and she loved the very real purple majesty of the mountains rising up in the distance to meet an azure sky. As much as she thought of this corner of the Arizona desert as being hers, it was always humbling to remember, as her history-loving father had loved pointing out to her, that much less than two hundred years ago everything she could see had been the undisputed domain of the Chiricahua Apaches.

Today, however, she didn't bother admiring the landscape. Her thoughts were focused on Junior Dowdle—a troubled individual with the body of a grown man, the ailments of an old one, and the heart and mind of a child. Knowing that Junior was out in the world somewhere—lost, alone, and unprotected—was heartbreaking, and she uttered a quiet prayer as she drove. "Please help us find him," she pleaded. "Please let him be okay."

Driving through the central business district of Old Bisbee on Tombstone Canyon Road, Joanna kept her eyes peeled, watching for anything out of the ordinary on side streets or on the steep scrub-oak-dotted hillsides that loomed above the town. If Junior had wandered outside in the dark, it wouldn't have taken him long to cross that narrow strip of civilization and find himself lost in a desert wilderness with neither food nor water.

Joanna had just passed Tombstone Canyon Methodist Church when her radio crackled to life.

"Alvin Bernard just called. Terry and Spike have arrived at the Maxwells' house. They're working on finding a scent. Everyone else is at St. Dom's."

"Okay," Joanna told Tica. "I'm almost there, too."

When Joanna arrived at the parking lot for St. Dominick's Catholic Church, she found Father Matthew Rowan, one of St. Dom's two resident priests, standing at the gate directing traffic. He pointed Joanna toward a clutch of official-looking vehicles. Tucked in among the collection of patrol cars sat a 1960s-era VW. The chaplain sticker on the VW Bug's back bumper explained its odd presence among the other official vehicles. The vintage VW belonged to Joanna's friend and pastor, the Reverend Marianne Maculyea, who in the past month had been certified as a chaplain for the local police and fire departments. It was no surprise to Joanna that, if first responders were on the scene, Marianne would be, too.

Pulling into the open spot next to the VW, Joanna stayed in the car for a moment, taking in the scene. The hustle and bustle might have been part of something as innocuous as a church bazaar. Cars came and went. The center of activity seemed to be a hastily erected eight-by-ten-foot canvas canopy. Some enterprising soul had used several matching sawhorses and a piece of plywood to create a massive makeshift table on which a six-foot-long paper map of the city had been tacked down. Surrounded by teams of officers and volunteers, Chief Bernard was bent over the map, assigning people to the streets and neighborhoods they were expected to search.

Twenty yards away from Chief Bernard's command center, a clutch of ladies from several nearby churches were setting up a refreshment buffet complete with a coffee urn, stacks of Styrofoam cups, and a surprising selection of store-bought and homemade baked goods and cookies. A blond teenage boy, someone Joanna didn't recognize, sprinted past her. Carrying a thermal coffee carafe in one hand, he waved in Joanna's direction with the other. Looking at her rather than at traffic, he came close to stepping into the path of another arriving vehicle.

"Look out!" Joanna called out, and he jumped back just in time.

Another stranger, a woman Joanna had never seen before, shouted after him, too. "For Pete's sake, Lucas! Watch what you're doing! Pay attention."

Joanna turned to the woman, a harried-looking thirty-something. Her long dirty-blond hair was pulled back in a scraggly ponytail. "He's yours?" Joanna asked.

When the woman nodded apologetically, a faint whiff of booze and an even stronger scent of cigarette smoke floated in Joanna's direction.

"My son," she answered, "fourteen years old and full of piss and vinegar. Once the coffee was ready, he wanted to be the one to take it to Chief Bernard." Then, glimpsing the badge and name tag on Joanna's uniform, the woman's eyes widened in recognition. "You're Sheriff Brady?"

Joanna nodded.

"I'm Rebecca Nolan. Lucas is my son. My daughter, Ruth, Lucas's twin sister, is over there."

The woman nodded toward the refreshment table. Following Rebecca's gaze, Joanna caught sight of a teenage girl who, with her mouth pursed in concentration, was laying out straight lines of treats in a carefully designed fashion. Rebecca had said the girl was Lucas's twin. True, they were about the same size—fair skinned and blue eyed—with features that were almost mirror images. They were also dressed in matching bright blue track suits. When it came to hair, though, the two kids weren't on the same page. Lucas's dark blond hair resembled his mother's. Ruth's, on the other hand, was mostly dyed deep purple, with a few natural blond strands showing through here and there. A glance at the girl's purple locks was enough to make Joanna grateful that her own daughter's hair didn't look like it came from a box of crayons.

"I hope you don't mind the kids being here," Rebecca added quickly. "I'm homeschooling them, and we've been doing a unit on community service. When I heard what happened, I told the kids to get their butts out of bed because we were coming down to help. I don't know Moe and Daisy well, but we live just up the street from them. It seemed like the right thing to do."

Marianne stepped into the conversation and handed Joanna a cup of coffee. "Good morning, Rebecca," she said cordially. "So glad you and the kids could make it."

Rebecca nodded. "I'd better go help," she said, backing away.

"You know her?" Joanna asked as Rebecca melted into the refreshment crowd.

"I met them at Safeway shortly after they arrived in town," Marianne said. "They've only been here a few months. Rebecca is divorced. Moved here from someplace in New Mexico with a boyfriend who disappeared almost as soon as they got to town."

"What does she do for a living?" Joanna asked.

Marianne shrugged. "I'm not sure, but she's homeschooling the two kids, which strikes me as a full-time job all its own. I know for a fact that I wouldn't be any good at homeschooling, and neither would Jeff." Jeff Daniels was Marianne's husband.

Joanna nodded. "The same goes for me," she agreed. "I've never been teacher material."

They stood for a moment, sipping their respective cups of coffee in the early morning cool and appreciating the quiet comfort of an enduring friendship that had started in junior high. Bisbee may not have boasted an official Welcome Wagon organization, but Reverend Maculyea filled the bill anyway. When it came to newcomers in town, you could count on Marianne to have a handle on them— where they came from, what they were about, and whether or not they needed any kind of assistance. Other people lived their lives by drawing circles in the sand designed to keep people out. Marianne's whole purpose in life was to draw circles that pulled people in.

"You got here fast," Joanna observed as another pair of cars nosed into the lot and parked where Father Rowan indicated. "I'm the sheriff. How come you got the call before I did?"

To anyone else, it might have sounded like a dig, but Marianne didn't take offense. "I wasn't called," she explained. "I heard it from Jeff. He went out for an early morning run up the canyon and came across Moe Maxwell, who was already out looking for Junior on his own. Jeff convinced Moe that he needed to call the cops, then came straight home and told me."

"You're the one who summoned all the ladies?" Joanna asked, nodding toward the gathering of women who were bustling around setting out tables and folding chairs.

Marianne grinned. "I didn't have to summon all of them," she replied. "All I had to do was call the first two people on my list. Each of those called two more. It's the first time we've used CCT," she added. "It worked like a charm."

For months, Marianne had been spearheading a team of local pastors and parishioners who had established something they called Christ's Crisis Tree, a phone tree organization that used a combination of text messages and landline calls to mobilize members of various churches to respond quickly to community emergencies, where they provided refreshments to all those involved, first responders and volunteers alike.

Marianne's grin faded as quickly as it had come. Joanna turned in time to see Daisy Maxwell, disheveled and distraught, coming toward them. Marianne hurried forward to embrace the woman.

"So sorry," Marianne said. "I'm sure they'll find him soon."

Daisy nodded numbly. "I hope so," she agreed. Then she turned to Joanna. "That guy from your department was up at the house, the one with the dog."

"Terry Gregovich," Joanna told her.

"Before I left, I gave him some of Junior's clothing so the dog would have his scent. I hope and pray it works. That's why Chief Bernard had everyone else, including these wonderful volunteers, meet here at the church instead of at our place. He didn't want people disrupting the scent and interfering with the dog."

"Spike's good at his job," Joanna said reassuringly. "Would you like some coffee, Daisy? Something to eat?"

That was what people did in difficult times—they offered food and drink. Daisy rejected both with a firm shake of her head, all the while gazing in wonder at the bustling parking lot.

"Where did all these people come from and how did they get here so fast?" she asked. "It's only a little past six. How did they even know what had happened?"

"They care about you," Marianne said, "and they care about Junior, too. Let's go sit down for a while."

Taking Daisy by the arm, Marianne led her to a nearby table. Meanwhile, Detective Matt Keller, a Bisbee police officer and Alvin Bernard's lead investigator, wandered over to the refreshment area and collected a cup of coffee before joining Joanna.

"Making any progress?" she asked.

Matt shook his head. "Not much. I've talked to all the people who live on O'Hara, the Maxwells' street," he said. "Because it was so warm last night almost all the neighbors had their windows open, but nobody seems to have heard or seen anything out of line, including Jack and Lois Radner, who live right next door. I talked to both of them and to their son, Jason, whose bedroom faces Junior's. So far I've got nothing that would help with timing, not even so much as a barking dog."

Joanna looked away from the detective in time to see two sheriff's department patrol vehicles nose into the parking lot. As she walked over to confer with her deputies, her phone rang and Terry Gregovich's name appeared in her caller ID.

"I could use some help up here," he said.

"Where are you? Did you find a scent?"

"We found one, all right. The trail from the house led up to the highway above town at milepost 337," he said. "We're there now. Spike may be able to follow the trail on the pavement or across the pavement, whichever it turns out to be, but we won't be able to do either one until we have someone up here to direct traffic."

"Two patrol deputies just arrived," Joanna told him. "I'll send them right up. You said milepost 337?"

"That's right," Terry confirmed.

"If somebody up on the highway gave Junior a ride, he could be miles away by now."

"I know," Terry said. "If the trail ends in the middle of the pavement, we'll know that's probably what happened."

Joanna hustled over to the two cars just as Deputies Ruiz and Stock stepped out of their vehicles. Deputy Stock's usual patrol area was on Highway 80 between Tombstone and Benson, while Deputy Ruiz spent most of his time on the stretch of Highway 92, west of Don Luis and out as far as the base of the Huachuca Mountains.

Joanna turned to Deputy Stock. "Did you see anyone walking on the highway as you came over the Divide?" she asked.

Jeremy shook his head. "Not a soul," he said. "Do we have any idea how long Junior's been gone?"

"Less than ten hours," Joanna said. "He took off sometime during the night. Right now, I need both of you up on the highway at milepost 337 to assist the K-9 unit. Spike picked up Junior's scent and followed it there. Before they can venture onto the pavement, they need someone directing traffic."

"On our way," Jeremy said. He turned to head out, but Joanna stopped him.

"No lights or sirens until you get there," she cautioned. "I don't want a hundred civilians milling around on the highway. One of them might get killed."

As the deputies hurried to do her bidding, Joanna went in search of Alvin Bernard. She wanted to tell him she had just heard from Terry Gregovich. To do so, she had to get in line behind one of her least favorite people, Marliss Shackleford, the *Bisbee Bee*'s intrepid reporter.

Marliss may have been Joanna's mother's closest chum, but she was also a gossipy busybody and the bane of Joanna's existence. Knowing that Marliss dished out the same kind of torment to Alvin Bernard made it only slightly less irksome to Joanna.

As soon as the reporter caught sight of Joanna, she registered her surprise. "How come you and your people are here, Sheriff Brady?" Marliss demanded abruptly. "My understanding is that Junior disappeared from the Maxwells' place on O'Hara. That's well inside the city limits and outside your jurisdiction. Isn't this whole circus a bit of an overreaction to someone simply wandering off?" She waved dismissively at the crowd of people milling in and out of the parking lot.

"Most of these folks are volunteers," Joanna told her. "My people are here because Chief Bernard requested my department's assistance, and we're happy to oblige. As for its being an overreaction? I doubt that's how Daisy Maxwell would characterize it. In fact, Daisy is right over there chatting with Marianne. Why don't you ask her?"

Marliss scurried off in search of Daisy Maxwell. "Thanks for getting rid of her," Alvin Bernard muttered once the reporter was safely out of earshot. "I was afraid she was going to be on my case all morning long."

Quickly Joanna briefed him on the situation with Terry and Spike.

"Should I call off the street search, then?" Chief Bernard asked.

"Not yet," Joanna replied. "Just because Junior wandered up to the highway doesn't mean he didn't come back down into town somewhere else. I sent a pair of uniformed deputies up there to direct traffic. What we don't need on the scene is a mob of civilians."

"You're right about that," Bernard agreed.

"Why don't I go see if I can assist my guys?" Joanna told him. "I'll call you directly if we find any sign of Junior."

When their conversation was interrupted by questions from someone else, Joanna took the opportunity to slip away. Once in her Yukon, she exited the parking lot, drove back down to Tombstone Canyon, and then headed north to the junction with Highway 80. Merging into the southbound lane, she turned on her light bar and flashers and drove slowly down the highway, scanning the shoulders on both sides of the road as she went. When she reached mileage marker 337, she pulled over to the side of the road and tucked in behind Deputy Stock's Ford Explorer.

"Where's Terry?" she asked.

"Up there," he said, pointing up the steep hillside above the highway. "He and Spike took off up that gully."

Years earlier, when the new highway bypass was built, the roadway had been carved out of the series of undulating limestone cliffs that covered the hillside. The mounds of cliffs were separated by steep gullies. During rainstorms those washes turned into cascades of fast-running water. Bone dry at the moment, they offered a natural but rough stairway leading up through otherwise impassable terrain. Pulling a pair of binoculars off her belt, Joanna scanned the mountainside.

When Anglos had first arrived in what was now south-eastern Arizona, the Mule Mountains had been covered by a forest of scrub oak. The trees had been cut down to provide firewood for home use as well as for smelting the copper being mined underground. As a girl, Joanna had hiked these hills with her father. Back then most of the scrub oak had been little more than overgrown bushes. Decades later those same slow-growing shrubs had matured into genuine trees, growing here and there in dense clusters.

Joanna was still scouring the hillside with her binoculars when Spike and Terry popped out from behind the cover of one of those groves of trees. They remained visible for only a matter of moments before resuming their climb and disappearing into another clump of scrub oak a few yards farther on. Even from this distance Joanna could see that Terry was struggling to keep up with his agile dog. Spike, nose to the ground and intent on his quarry, lunged forward with his brushy tail plumed out behind him.

Joanna knew that Terry Gregovich prided himself on being in top physical condition. If this was proving to be a tough climb for him, how had Junior managed it? The missing man was in his early sixties. He was naturally clumsy and anything but a natural athlete. Joanna was hard-pressed to imagine Junior making the same climb, especially alone and in the dark. Still, she also understood that the trail didn't lie. Junior's scent had to be there because that's what Spike was following.

"Did there happen to be a full moon last night?" Joanna asked.

"Yes, ma'am, there was," Deputy Stock answered. "Out between here and Tombstone it was almost as bright as day."

Just then Joanna heard the dog. Spike's excited, purposeful barks alerted everyone within earshot that he had located his target. Almost a minute later, Terry reappeared, popping out of the second grove of trees. As Deputy Gregovich came into view, Joanna's phone rang.

"I found him," Terry said urgently.

"Where?" Joanna asked. "Is he all right?"

"I can't tell if he's all right or not," Terry replied. "I can see him, but I can't reach him. I called to him, but he didn't respond. He doesn't appear to be breathing."

"Where is he?"

"At the bottom of a glory hole inside a cave of some kind. I always heard rumors about a series of limestone caverns under the mountain, but I never really believed it. The narrow opening that leads into it is hidden in the trees directly behind me."

Joanna knew that the Mule Mountains were riddled with natural caverns and man-made glory holes—small test holes that had been drilled into the earth by prospectors and left abandoned when no ore was found.

"Which is it?" Joanna asked, "a glory hole or a cave?"

"A little of both," Terry replied. "The cave itself is natural, but there's a small glory hole inside it that someone must have worked for a while. The tailings outside the entrance are hidden under the trees. If I'd been on my own, I would have missed the opening completely. Fortunately, Spike didn't. Someone put an iron grate across the entrance to keep people out. Junior evidently crawled under it. So did Spike and I. The glory hole is a few feet inside the cave, and it's a big drop-off. I can see Junior facedown at the bottom of that, lying on top of a layer of loose rock and boulders where it looks like the side of the hole collapsed. There's a cat or kitten stuck down there, too. It's on an outcropping halfway between where I was and where Junior is. I can't see it, but I can hear it crying. I'll bet that's what happened. Junior was following the kitten, and they both fell."

"Can you get to him?" Joanna asked.

"Not me, not without ropes and a winch."

"Okay," Joanna said. "I'm on it. Calling for help right now."

About the Author

J. A. JANCE is the New York Times bestselling author of the J. P. Beaumont series, the Joanna Brady series, the Ali Reynolds series, and four interrelated thrillers about the Walker family, as well as a volume of poetry. Born in South Dakota and brought up in Bisbee, Arizona, Jance lives with her husband in Seattle, Washington, and Tucson, Arizona.

www.jajance.com

Visit www.AuthorTracker.com for exclusive information on your favorite HarperCollins authors.